CHL

jP 8537 sh
Potter
The shared room

W9-BJV-000

ESLC90

Children's

DENVER
PUBLIC LIBRARY

FINE FOR OVERTIME

DEMCO

DATE DUE
11 1 .87
E DUE
8 24 .87

R01093 71378

THE SHARED ROOM

THE
SHARED
ROOM

by
Marian Potter

DENVER
PUBLIC LIBRARY

SEP '80

CITY & COUNTY OF DENVER

William Morrow and Company New York 1979

R01093 71378

Copyright © 1979 by Marian Potter

All rights reserved. No part of this book may be reproduced or
utilized in any form or by any means, electronic or mechanical,
including photocopying, recording or by any information storage
and retrieval system, without permission in writing from the
Publisher. Inquiries should be addressed to William Morrow
and Company, Inc., 105 Madison Ave., New York, N. Y. 10016.

Library of Congress Cataloging in Publication Data

Potter, Marian.
    The shared room.

    Summary: Despite her grandmother's opposition, a 10-year-
old reestablishes contact with her long-institutionalized mother.
    [1. Mentally ill—Fiction. 2. Mothers and daughters—Fiction.
3. Grandmothers—Fiction] I. Title.
PZ7.P853Sh [Fic] 79-18012
ISBN 0-688-22209-9
ISBN 0-688-32209-3 lib. bdg.

Printed in the United States of America.

1 2 3 4 5 6 7 8 9 10

jP
8537
sh

1

Catherine reread the paragraph she had written: "I can just barely remember the plane that brought us from Iraq, where I was born. I was left in St. Stephen while my mother flew on to Seattle, Washington, with all our money in a tote bag. My life would have been different if the plane had not crashed. My mother was killed, and all our money shredded up."

She studied the top of the page where she had filled in the blanks: title Autobiography of Catherine Doyle, age 10, grade 5, date Sept. 21, 1973.

Her name looked mighty plain. She wished she had a nickname, something cute like Bobbi, the girl who sat across the aisle. She erased "Catherine" and wrote "Katheryn." That helped some.

The heavy black of her felt-tip pen looked better than the faded purple of the mimeographed form brought in by Ms. Rosengren, the elementary counselor. You'd think she was the teacher instead of Mr. Buford Beaumont from the way she took over his desk. She said she needed it for her presentation.

Catherine wanted to dash off more bold, black words about herself, but first she needed to know more about Ms. Rosengren. She wondered how long she'd lived in St. Stephen. Bobbi Clark would know. She knew all that stuff. Bobbi was not only her neighbor at school, but at home, too. She lived in the same block. There was no way Catherine could get away from Bobbi.

Bobbi finished her work and bobbed up to Ms. Rosengren, waving her sheet. Without seeing it, Catherine knew it began, "My name is Roberta. I'm named for my father."

Ms. Rosengren nodded. "Very good. Class, Bobbi has finished her autobiography. That's commendable." Ms. Rosengren continued to nod. Words didn't flow from her lips; they got spit out. She called it "enunciation" and sort of peeled her teeth when she talked.

"I want to emphasize that this will help your orientation," she enunciated, "when you eventually go to the middle-school level. Your autobiography will be placed on file with the occupational-apti-tude-and-preference test you have completed. This year you will continue to research your career goals."

Bryan Jones fell over his big feet lurching up to the front of the room. Light shone through his big ears. If commendables were being passed out, he wanted to get his. He counted out the pages to show Ms. Rosengren he had written four. Bryan had this big IQ his mother told everybody about. Maybe big ears and big feet went with a big IQ.

Since Bobbi had finished her autobiography, she could go to any of the interest centers in the room, which was as big as a skating rink. She skipped over to the science center, not because she cared a bean sprout about science, but because she was bothered if the center was messy. Bobbi liked to wash the dirty flasks the other kids had left and to put the place in order.

Catherine took her unfinished sheet and joined Bobbi. "I've already done my career goals, too," Bobbi said, as she placed clean flasks neatly on shelves.

"I know, beautician like your mother."

"I'm going to have my own shop and be boss."

"I think I'll take aviator," Catherine said.

"Aviator? Last year you took archeologist. Don't you want to be that anymore?"

"Oh, I never wanted to be an archeologist. A's come first on the list. I just look at the top of the list and pick one. First I'll have to finish my auto-biography, though." She put flasks on the top shelf, for she was much taller than Bobbi. "I think Ms. Rosengren should write her autobiography for us. Do you know anything about her?"

"Sure. My mom says she used to come to our shop a long time ago. Now she's coming again because she's got this job and can't go around looking like a peeled onion. What's it to you?"

"Nothing," Catherine answered. In a way that was true. There was nothing more she needed to know. So Ms. Rosengren had lived in St. Stephen a long time. That meant she probably knew more about Catherine than Catherine knew about herself. It was unfair, and it made her uneasy.

"You won't see much of her unless you act up," Bobbi went on. "She told my mom she's finished a lot of extra college work and got this job so she could have an office with a bunch of files instead of a classroom with a bunch of kids." Bobbi sniffed a jar. "Look at these alfalfa seeds. All moldly. Clean this up."

"Not now," Catherine said. She paused at each interest center on her way to the big desk. Even though Ms. Rosengren was an ordinary person who went to Bobbi's mother's beauty shop, Catherine always felt a little scared when she talked to a teacher. A counselor might be worse. She took a deep breath. "I don't want to finish my auto-biography today," she blurted out.

Ms. Rosengren nodded. "Very well, that's understandable. I can be flexible to allow you more time. Flexibility for the individual is important. I must be off to other fifth grades to make presentations. Most of you have finished. If you have not, give your work to Mr. Beaumont when it is complete. He, in turn, will see that I receive it for your comprehensive file. Remember, it is important for your orientation."

She gathered up her papers, gave several final nods, and left. Could be, Catherine thought, she wouldn't read late autobiographies. She might just put them in her file.

Diane couldn't keep quiet any longer. She fluttered her hand. "Mr. Beaumont, is orientation something about China and Japan and like that?"

Mr. Beaumont pointed to the dictionary on its special stand. "Diane, I suggest you consult Big Web."

Diane didn't seem to mind when Bryan Jones laughed at her. She just pushed back that long hair of hers, which looked like an unraveled rope, and laughed with him. Diane was a kind-of friend of Catherine's. She, too, lived on the same street.

Mr. Beaumont didn't supply answers as much as he told kids where they could find them themselves.

He was the only man teacher in South Range Elementary, and he did a lot of things differently. Never mind all those Maypole hey-nonney songs, he said, and put aside the records the music teacher had left. He brought in his own records, and his guitar, too.

When they started an art project, they finished it, although Bobbi hated to have their room messed up for a whole week.

Scott Norton, who was a nature freak, could bring in any bird's-nest, cocoon, or sick plant. Once he brought in a chicken egg, and it hatched right in the middle of division of fractions.

Eric Huskey was such a pack rat that stuff in his pockets nearly pulled off his pants. When he brought in some piece of junk he'd found, Mr. Beaumont stood back, admired it, and said, "Beautiful, beautiful."

He didn't sit at his desk very much. As he got up, Catherine followed him to the verbal-arts center. "Mr. Beaumont, will you read these autobiographies before you give them to Ms. Rosengren for her file?"

"I might rake my eyes over some, should time allow. Since I am new this autumn in your fair city, it would be a way to get better acquainted."

It was a great chance. She could make up more about herself. Mr. Beaumont wouldn't know the difference; he was new in St. Stephen. Still, that might not be fair to him. Besides, he was awful smart. He might see right through that pack of lies she'd started to write. On her way back to her seat, Catherine crumpled the paper she was holding and tossed it in the wastebasket.

2

After school Bobbi and Catherine started home. Above the shouts of many children, they heard a shriek.

Bobbi sighed. "That's Diane. We have to wait for her."

"Why?"

"My mom said I have to walk home with her. Diane's mother gets her hair done at our shop every week. She gets a high tease and a French twist."

When she caught up with them, Diane was breathless. "I saw you!" she squealed at Catherine. "I saw you throw away your autobiography, and that was special too."

Catherine shrugged. "Big deal. I don't like to write about myself."

"Oh, I do," Bobbi said. "It's my favorite subject."

"Every fall we have to do those family things," Catherine said. "We started in first grade when our teacher was Miss Small."

"Her name was Miss Little," Bobbi corrected her.

"Well, I know we made a book because Nana let me keep mine."

"Nana! You ought to call her Grandma, like she is." Bobbi was great at correcting.

Diane's house was first, then Bobbi's. Catherine's was the last in the block.

Her house was like all the other frame houses she knew in St. Stephen. Nana claimed there had been one busy contractor in town, and he built all his houses in just the same way. The front door opened into the living room, an open stairway went upstairs to the right, and a doorway straight ahead led to the kitchen. Nana had tried to make a pretend hall by placing a long rug and a skinny table beside the stairway.

When Catherine opened the front door, she heard the whirring of the Singer portable. Through the wide arch opening on the left of the living room she could see into the dining room, where her grandmother was sewing at the big table.

Nana cut threads and looked up. "Hi, hon, you home already? Seems like you just left."

Catherine went into the dining room and stood

beside the table. Nana always looked worried when she sewed. There was a big frown wrinkle above her nose that didn't show so much at any other time. She guided a strip of pink fabric under the needle, and a long pink ruffle began to grow faster than Jack's beanstalk. "I'm using the ruffler first time. Tricky business."

"What's that for?"

"For that pink check of yours. This ruffle sewed on the bottom will make that dress long enough."

"I don't want it."

"What?" Nana stopped sewing. The frown mark was deeper than ever. She took off her glasses and rubbed her eyes.

"I want to wear pants and tops like the other kids. Mr. Beaumont wouldn't care. Be practical, be comfortable, he says. I sure am glad I'm in his room."

"We'll see about that. As for being practical, what's more saving than making do with outgrown dresses? You're growing so. Of course, you come by it natural."

"From my mother or my father? Which one is so tall?"

"Oh, I was thinking about *my* father, your great grandpa Highfield."

"It's all right for us to know all about your father, but what about mine, Nana?"

14

"The least said about him, the better." Nana dropped the machine presser foot and raced the machine.

"At school we're supposed to write about ourselves and our families." Catherine raised her voice to be heard above the machine. "Shall I say my father took off like a big-assed bird?"

Nana jerked the machine to a stop. "Now look here. I don't believe I really heard what I thought I did. You just keep a civil tongue in your head. When you write at school, just say your mother is sick. That's the truth. We've always told you so. You don't have to write anything about your father."

"But what if I want to? Maybe I just want to, you know."

Just then the back door banged. Tin rattled. Pop was home from work with his empty lunch bucket. He'd be tired and not want to hear a lot of fuss.

"That you, Thurman?" Nana called.

Catherine's grandfather came to the dining-room door. "You expecting somebody else?"

Pop was a machinist at Castex. He wore coveralls there over his plaid flannelette shirt and corduroy pants, but he brought the smell of metal and oil home with him all the same.

Of the three plants in St. Stephen, Castex was the biggest and hired the most people. Its long, low, metal buildings at the end of River Street were mysterious to Catherine. She didn't know what Pop made on the machines there, for Castex was a plant that made things for other plants. Nana didn't know much about Castex either, except that they were lucky it was in St. Stephen. Lots of towns in western New York didn't have plants at all.

Catherine could tell how tired Pop was from the droop of his shoulders. Nana looked at him intently as if he reminded her of something. "I forgot to thaw any meat for supper. I declare, I get started on my sewing, time goes by, and I forget. Not that my sewing does any good." A whine started in her voice. "It's not worth the fuss of getting the ruffler on the machine. She says she doesn't want it, after I work the livelong day. And deviling me again about things. Comes home with a lot of vulgar talk. . . ." Nana began to cry.

"Now, Betty, sewing makes you nervous." Pop patted her on the shoulder. "It always did. Won't matter if supper is a little late. I've got things to do in the shop, like paint the frames of the storm windows before they go up. Just give a holler when soup's on."

"Wouldn't you know it? The bobbin has run out." Nana sniffed as she gathered up scraps of pink cloth.

Catherine had no shop to escape to, but she had her room upstairs. From the window she watched

16

Pop walk wearily across the yard to the little building beside the garage. It hadn't been a very nice homecoming for him. She'd only been in the house a few minutes before she'd had Nana bawling. Now she didn't feel very good either.

She loved Pop and Nana and was sorry she'd made Nana cry. Without them, she wouldn't have anyone to take care of her. She might even be dead and have a gravestone with a little lamb on it. Still, she wanted to know more about her own parents, not about how poor Nana had been growing up on that old hill farm before she moved into St. Stephen.

In this room she felt especially close to her mother, for it had once been hers. Sometimes Nana forgot and called it "Kathleen's room." Catherine was most reminded of her mother when she sat before the dressing table with its little drawers on each side. There was a dusting of face powder in the drawer corners, and bobby pins were in the cracks. Nana had taken away other reminders. Bright squares on the faded wallpaper showed where pictures had hung.

But Nana had overlooked three big, heavy books on the high shelf of the closet. Catherine would soon be able to reach that shelf without standing on the dressing-table chair.

From under those books she pulled out sheets

of faded colored paper stapled together. They were the *My Family* book she'd made in first grade. The people she had drawn looked awful dumb, floating between blue-crayon streaks of sky and green-crayon streaks of grass.

She remembered the teacher had wanted her to label two of the figures Grandmother and Grandfather, but she'd insisted on Nana and Pop. She had left a blank page to be filled in for Father. It was still blank.

Even then she had known her mother was sick, so she had drawn a lady in bed and a nurse and doctor beside the bed. The teacher had liked the picture.

Catherine had decided to make the same picture on a card to send to her mother. Under the picture she had printed "Get Well Quick." The card was still in the back of the book. Nana had never told her where to send it.

Of course, she knew better than to send a corny card like that now that she was in fifth grade. She replaced it inside the back cover. Someday she and her mother would have a good laugh over it here in their shared room.

3

For a whole week Catherine did not see Ms. Rosengren around school. She was probably off somewhere with her files and would never bug Catherine for that autobiography.

Not so with Miss Henrietta Kneehoff. You couldn't get in or out of South Range Elementary without her inspection. As Catherine loitered by the big glass door at the school entrance, she could see Miss Kneehoff standing straight as a flagpole in front of her office door. She was now principal; before she'd been Catherine's second-grade teacher.

Far from the door, where Miss Kneehoff could neither see nor hear them, some kids limped around, saying Henry had et their knees off.

Miss Kneehoff wore a flowered knit dress, the kind Nana wore to church. Her hair was reddish mixed with gray, which made it a faded pink. That was the color Nana liked for Catherine's dresses. Miss Kneehoff's eyes, enlarged behind the thick lenses of her glasses, were such a watery, pale blue that it was a wonder they were good for seeing. But she saw plenty. She often popped into classrooms for surprise inspections.

It seemed to Catherine that Miss Kneehoff had a special way of looking at her. Catherine decided to test her impression. As she passed the office in the midst of a pack of kids, she glanced up at Miss Kneehoff. Sure enough, the principal's blank, nonseeing eyes lighted up a little, and she smiled slightly.

Catherine did not know why she was so regarded. Maybe Miss Kneehoff thought Catherine was special because she had learned to read so well in the second grade.

Actually Nana's cousin Ted was the one who had taught her to read, and he didn't even know it. Miss Kneehoff had started the year by telling them they would learn consonants and vowels. If you knew those sounds, you could read anything. Consonants weren't so bad, but vowels were awful. Each one had at least two different sounds. Some of them were like the grunts and groans that came from the speech-correction class. Then, by chance, Catherine had found the key when Cousin Ted had stayed with them.

Nana had said it was just a downright shame that Cousin Ted couldn't find work around Burnt Timbers where he lived. Pop said Cousin Ted's appearance was against him; he was so fat he looked like a loose load of hay coming down the road. Nana had invited him to stay with them and look for work in St. Stephen.

Nana had shopped for groceries more carefully than ever, which wasn't easy with prices high as a cat's back. She had read all the labels on the cereal boxes and said there was no way you could beat oatmeal.

Each morning Nana had cooked oatmeal for Pop, Catherine, and Cousin Ted. One morning Catherine had taken a spoonful of hot oatmeal without blowing on it. She had shifted it around in her mouth like a shortstop fielding a ball.

"Where's Ted?" Nana had asked. "His oatmeal is hot. Where's Ted?"

Her mouth full of hot oatmeal, Catherine said, "Fat Ted is not up." It came out, "*a, e, i, o, u.*" She was amazed. She had sounded like Miss Kneehoff's vowels.

"Don't speak with your mouth full," Nana said.

Catherine took a drink of cold milk and finished her breakfast. On the way to school she practiced saying, "Fat Ted is not up," with her mouth open. She was the first one called on for flash-card drill.

Although she was a little slow, she said all the vowels correctly.

Both Catherine and Miss Kneehoff were surprised. Miss Kneehoff said it just proved that the short sounds of the vowels were easy to master, even for someone like Catherine, whatever that meant.

Bobbi was not impressed. She was kind of sore at Catherine and said she hated vowels and second grade. So Catherine told her the fat-Ted secret and made her promise not to tell Bryan Jones.

But he soon learned vowel sounds anyhow; and, sure enough, he could read anything. They never did tell Diane, and she was still trying to catch up.

Cousin Ted didn't get a lick of work and went home to Burnt Timbers to eat buttered hot cakes and syrup for breakfast.

That had been a long time ago; but as Catherine went into her fifth-grade classroom, she thought of how lucky Ted's visit had been for her. She would hate to be a stumbling reader for a teacher like Mr. Beaumont.

That morning, however, Mr. Beaumont was concerned with how well they could speak. He held up a big, floppy book. "I see by this syllabus that we are supposed to have a unit on Being a Worthy Home Member. Now let's meet that requirement and get on to something we think up ourselves."

He turned a page. "Here are some topics for oral expression. That means you get up here and talk. How about this one:—The Best Thing My Family Did for Me Last Summer and the Best Thing I Did for My Family? Groans will get you nowhere. We'll start tomorrow."

Catherine wanted to be ready. When she stood in front of the class, she wanted to speak right up like Barbara Walters. She didn't want to *um* and *ah* and giggle the way Diane did.

She remembered June 21, the longest day of the year, when Nana and Pop had let her sleep out in the yard. That could be the best thing her family had done for her. One summer day she had made Nana laugh so hard she had to take off her glasses and wipe her eyes. She held her sides because they ached so. Pop had laughed, too, seeing Nana so tickled. That didn't happen very often. Catherine thought it was the best thing she had done for her family.

But Bobbi said you couldn't tell about things like that. They had to last longer, like a trip in a recreational vehicle or going to Washington, D. C. As the best thing she'd done for her family, Bobbi planned to tell of taking out all the crud around the bathroom tiles.

Catherine wasn't called on the first day and was still thinking of what to say when her turn came.

She had a crawly feeling in her stomach when she began. "My mother and father wanted to take me to Virginia Beach. They wanted us all to go to the ocean where we could swim and sun on the beach every day."

The classroom door opened just wide enough to let Miss Kneehoff slip in. Catherine stopped. If she'd known Miss Kneehoff would hear, she'd have made up a different summer. But she had started, and even Diane was listening. So she went on.

"It's a long ways, and right at the beginning, our old Chevy broke down. Our cousin Ted, he's fat. He has a car, so he took us. He can drive all right, but he can't tell where he's going. So I had the map, and I read the signs and told him when the exit was coming and when we got to it. We didn't make one single mistake and went right to the nice house we rented on the beach."

Catherine no longer felt scared. She began to enjoy her own talk. "Some days we went to a horse farm. Cousin Ted didn't go; he hates horses. It was just my mother and father on bay horses and mine was an Appaloosa. We rode all over this big horse farm and through woods."

Catherine told of other vacation joys and ended with a description of the seafood meals she had prepared for her family.

Bryan Jones had gone to Albany for three days.

You'd think he'd been around the world. When he finished, it was time for dismissal.

Miss Kneehoff stood at the door as the children filed out. She put her hand on Catherine's shoulder and drew her aside. "Come to the office for a minute."

That anxious, crawly feeling was back in Catherine's stomach as she followed Miss Kneehoff to her office. She waited while Miss Kneehoff saw all the kids through the big door. Suddenly the building was strangely quiet.

Miss Kneehoff sat down at her desk and motioned to Catherine to come stand beside her. "Were you just pretending about the summer?" she asked. Catherine looked into those eyes that didn't seem to see. "Can't you answer me?" There was no special kindly look from those eyes now. Miss Kneehoff must have forgotten what a good reader she was. "I know children often pretend, but we all have to keep straight what is real and what is pretend. Was it real?"

Catherine did not answer. You'd think she was in St. Stephen Courthouse being tried for something. She didn't understand why she was being questioned. The talk was for oral expression. How you said the words mattered more than what they were. She'd spoken right up. It wasn't fair to keep her after school. She looked out the window. Diane was chasing Bryan Jones. She longed to be outside running through the fallen leaves.

"I won't keep you long. I know your grandmother would be worried if you came home late." So now she knew what worried Nana, which was plenty. "Did you really go to the seashore with your parents last summer?"

Catherine said nothing.

Miss Kneehoff looked at her calendar. "Let's see. Yes, the elementary counselor will be in our building tomorrow. I think you should have a conference with Ms. Rosengren. Maybe you would feel more like talking with someone you don't see every day. Now run along."

Catherine didn't feel like running now. Her legs, heavy as logs, ached as she walked slowly toward home. Bobbi was in her yard, raking leaves with her mother. She dropped her rake and ran to Catherine. "I waited and even Diane waited so we could know what Miss Kneehoff wanted. What was it?"

"Oh, nothing."

Bobbi's mother raked quickly, the way she combed out a head of hair. "Miss Kneehoff takes her new job seriously. She hasn't changed except in looks. I remember when she was a stunning redhead."

"You do!" Catherine exclaimed.

"Sure, she was my second-grade teacher, you know, and your mo— Well, she was second-grade teacher for just about everyone in south St. Stephen."

"Here, we've got an extra." Bobbi thrust a rake into Catherine's hands. "We're going to get these all cleaned up today."

Catherine raked and thought. Nana had never told her how long Miss Kneehoff had been a teacher. Maybe in second grade she'd been too dumb to ask. Miss Kneehoff knew all about everybody in St. Stephen. Like Ms. Rosengren, Henrietta Kneehoff knew more about her than she knew about herself.

Maybe that's why she looked so kindly at her. But Miss Kneehoff wouldn't do that anymore, not after she'd heard her orally expressing first-class lies. Doubtless, she knew that Catherine Doyle had never seen the ocean and never been on a horse.

Catherine wished Miss Kneehoff had expelled her from school, had had her arrested, had done anything except tell her to see the elementary counselor, Ms. Nodding Noodle. She knew some kids who had to go talk with Ms. Rosengren every week; she didn't want to be one of them.

4

Next day, as Catherine went down the school hall, she thought of one of Nana's expressions, "It's not what you want but what you get that makes you fat." Catherine didn't want a counseling session, but she was sure going to get one. Ms. Rosengren waited in an alcove off the nurse's office and nodded Catherine into a chair at a low table opposite her desk.

She gave Catherine some papers to mark. They were like workbook pages, yes and no. While Catherine marked mostly *yes*, Ms. Rosengren marked some papers of her own. Then she brought out some things she called games, but they weren't any fun. Catherine was supposed to play these games by herself.

When she finished, Ms. Rosengren began to ask

her questions. Since Catherine didn't know what she was supposed to answer, she thought it best to say nothing. Blab, blab could be a big mistake.

"Well, if you don't wish to communicate just yet, I may as well do some of these other evaluations." Ms. Rosengren nodded as she began to write.

Catherine heard conversation in the nurse's office. A kid had thrown up. The nurse called his mother to come take him home. Afterward it was so quiet in the alcove that she could hear Ms. Rosengren's ball-point pen whisper over the paper. The electric clock on the wall buzzed. She put her head down on the table and had a good nap.

It hadn't been so bad. Catherine thought her counseling was finished. A week later she was surprised when Miss Kneehoff poked her head into the classroom and said, "Mr. Beaumont, you neglected to send Catherine to the conference room."

So there she was again, going down the hall to see Ms. Rosengren. If sitting there was ever going to end, she guessed she'd have to say that her mother was sick. That's all she could tell about her family unless she made something up, and making up stuff had got her there in the first place.

The nurse smiled when she went in. "You're all right, I hope."

"No, I'm sick," Catherine heard herself saying.

She rubbed her arm. "I had this flu shot yesterday after school, and my head hurts, and I think I'm going to throw up."

The nurse felt her forehead. "You're cool as a cucumber, but you might have some reaction from the shot. Does your grandmother have transportation?"

"Yes, but Pop takes it to work. I walk to school. I can walk home."

"We're not allowed to let a sick child go home alone."

"Bobbi Clark's mother lives close to us. She could come get me if she isn't doing a head of hair."

Nana was just dumbfounded to see Sue Clark bring Catherine home.

"You seem perfectly well to me. I've got a good notion to call Henrietta and see what they thought was wrong," she said, when Mrs. Clark left.

"No, Nana, don't call her, please. She hates calls. Interruptions all the time. . . . I've heard her say that. I'll get over whatever it is I've got. A lot of stuff is going around."

Catherine went upstairs and tried to lie still on her bed. Her head did hurt just a little from puzzling over how she'd managed to get there. Her stomach was perfectly level, not upset a bit. She had a brief nap and then heard Pop come in from work. In a little while she saw smoke coming from the tin-pipe chimney of his shop. It was cozy there when he fired up his wood stove.

"Nana, I'm feeling better, I think," Catherine called downstairs. "I'm going out to see Pop."

"Mighty quick recovery," Nana said, as Catherine dashed through the kitchen.

The door to the shop had a neat latch with a little hollow that just fit the thumb to push down. There was a glass window in the door with a curtain pushed aside. Pop said if there was one window in hell, Nana would try to hang an asbestos rag over it.

Catherine clicked open the latch. The workshop smelled of sawdust and varnish. Pop was standing sorting lengths of lumber and Masonite. "I thought you were under the weather," he said.

"I got well, and I felt like talking to somebody who doesn't carry around a clipboard and put everything in a file."

Pop smiled and started sorting molding. Although Catherine had always talked to him, he wasn't much of a talker. At Castex, where he worked, the big machines made so much noise that he had lost the talking habit. But she knew he'd listen and think about what she wanted him to know.

She watched him rule an edge on a piece of wood. "I'll bet that's for a present. Are you going to make Christmas presents this year?"

"Oh, might."

"Don't make me any. I don't want any presents this year," Catherine announced.

"You'll change your tune before snow flies," Pop said.

"All I want is to go visit my sick mother in the hospital or wherever she is."

Pop sat down in his old oak rocker. His big hands, hard and polished from working on oily machines, lay idle on each corduroy knee. "What you're asking for wouldn't be a present."

"Why, has she got something catching?"

"No," Pop said firmly, "and don't you ever let anybody tell you she has."

"Then I want to see her."

"It's understandable you'd want to visit her. I know that. You're getting older. Time goes so fast." Pop stroked her dark hair. There wasn't much to stroke. Nana thought long hair should be braided, not flying around collecting tangles. Braiding took too much time, so Nana had Mrs. Clark give Catherine a forty-five-degree taper cut.

"Are people allowed to see my mother?" Catherine asked.

"Yes, you could visit her, but it would only make you sad."

"I could stand to be sad, Pop. It would be better than being mad, the way I am now sometimes."

Pop reached out and pushed the curtain on the glass door farther aside. He looked out at the bare tree limbs outlined against the gray sky.

"You aren't going to bawl the way Nana does, are you, Pop? She begins to cry when I ask her things."

"I know. Her tears are a strong weapon. Just a little salt water, though."

"Then why do you come out here to get away from them?"

"Do I do that? Well, Nana's been through a lot, and I feel like a whipped dog when she's miserable. Besides, I made her a promise."

"What promise?"

"You'll know when you're old enough to understand."

"When will that be? Is it a certain birthday, like the year you have to start paying full admission at the movies?"

"No, some things don't go by age like that. Nana says we're not keeping anything from you. You know the truth—your mother is sick. It's enough for now."

It wasn't really enough, but Catherine knew Pop was done talking as he turned on the switch of his noisy table saw.

5

On the way to school the next morning Bobbi told Catherine there had been an awful to-do among Mr. Beaumont, Miss Kneehoff, Ms. Rosengren, and the school nurse because Catherine had got sick somewhere between the classroom and the conference room and was sent home.

"How did it come out?"

"I think they decided to wait and see if you were all right today. But you better watch it. Don't try any more tricks."

"I won't. I'll just go in and tell Mr. Beaumont I'm okay."

"We're going to plan a Halloween party today," Bobbi said. "Mr. Beaumont wants some mothers and fathers to come help."

Catherine wanted to be as straightforward with Mr. Beaumont as he was with the class. She'd tell him why her mother couldn't help with the party. Of course, she could volunteer Nana's help in serving refreshments; but she really didn't want Mr. Beaumont to see that Nana had gray hair, couldn't read without her glasses, and didn't wear slacks like the other mothers. Besides, Nana might look over the top of her glasses and find whatever it was she was always saying they were going to see about.

As the class talked about plans for the coming party, Mr. Beaumont strode around the room. Catherine followed him, and Diane trailed after Catherine. To get his attention, Catherine pulled on his sleeve. "Mr. Beaumont, I can bring a batch of brownies. I'll make them myself, not from a mix, either."

"Good, good," Mr. Beaumont said.

"But my mother can't help. She doesn't work like some of the others; she's sick."

"Well, let's hope she is well by All Hallowed Evening."

"No, she's sick all the time."

Softly Diane repeated the word *sick*. Catherine looked around to see Diane turning her pointed index finger around and around beside her head. The rest of the class saw her too.

Catherine ducked into her seat. If only she could

sink out of sight and vanish from that room. She stared at the cover of her math book as if she had never seen it before. When she opened it, the print danced around. The sight of tumbling words and numbers scared her. She felt panicky, as if she had to run out of the room. Gripping the sides of her desk, she tried to swallow whatever it was in her throat that wouldn't go down.

So that's the kind of sick it was, or so Diane thought. Diane! What did that creep know? She was mistaken, just as she was most of the time when she waved her hand to give wrong answers.

The bell rang, and Mr. Beaumont rose to take the class to the library. As the group moved down the hall, Catherine sidled up beside Diane. "Pants-on-fire liar," she muttered.

"I am not!" Diane declared.

"Are too," Catherine insisted.

"Am not."

"Are too!" Catherine repeated.

Bobbi fell in step beside them. "Not 'are too'. You should say 'are so.'"

Catherine brushed Bobbi aside like an annoying fly. "Oh, shut up!"

Bobbi sucked air through her teeth. "I don't like to be told to shut up." She hurried into the library after the rest of the class.

"You better watch out telling barefaced lies, Diane," Catherine threatened.

"I didn't tell any. You're the one telling them. It's the truth, or you wouldn't care."

"You shut up, pants-on-fire!"

Diane made a face. "I won't, and I'll tell you something else—it runs in families. There's streaks of it in families!" Diane darted into the library.

"May I help you, miss?" Mr. Beaumont saw Catherine standing just inside the door. "We have books for free on just about everything from abacus to zodiac." Catherine shook her head. Mr. Beaumont looked at her more closely. "Are you all right? Do you think you've got another reaction from that shot?"

"No, Mr. Beaumont," Catherine said quietly. "I didn't finish the book I got last library period. May I go back to our room?"

The won't-go-down feeling in her throat continued the rest of the afternoon. When she tried to take a deep breath, the air stuck and wouldn't go down deep in her chest the way it was supposed to. Breathing was most difficult when she thought of families with streaks.

Catherine didn't know just how the trouble started out on the sidewalk after school. Maybe

37

Diane, walking behind her, made that head-pointing gesture again. Catherine heard someone say, "Sick up here."

"Looney," a voice yelled.

Others chimed in. "Nuts, bonkers."

"Bats in the belfry. A few buttons missing." That was Eric Huskey.

"Gone bananas." Diane shrieked with laughter. "Crazy as a bedbug."

"Stop it! Stop it!" Bobbi yelled. "Leave her alone."

Catherine dropped her books and covered her ears, but she could still hear the taunts—out to lunch, light out in the upper story.

Bobbi looked helpless. Then a sly smile slid over her face, and she joined the others. "Off her rocker."

Something shook Catherine. It was like the jolt she had felt once when she had caught her thumb in a light socket. Feeling like the strongest girl in the world, she hit Eric Huskey in the stomach so hard that junk fell out of his pockets. Bryan Jones was too tall to hit, but she gave him a bone cracking kick in the shins. She got a handful of Diane's hair and pulled hard. Scott Norton dodged, but not soon enough. He got a good clout too. She bit somebody.

Bobbi ran yelling for Mr. Beaumont.

"Break it up, break it up!" Mr. Beaumont pushed through the ring of children around Catherine.

"Now what do we have here? What do we have here?" He held Catherine's flailing arms at her sides. "Do we have Miss Catherine Doyle, or do we have champion fighter Muhammad Ali?"

He sat her down on the curb beside him. "Now just try to get hold of yourself. You're shaking like a dog in a wet sack. Come inside, Ali, and get calmed down. Tell me about all this."

She pulled away. "No, no, I want to go home. I'm all right. I'm not allowed to get home late." Mr. Beaumont let her go.

Bobbi and Diane were a block farther down the street. Catherine walked slowly so that they would stay ahead. With a runny nose and red eyes, she didn't want to walk with them. Besides, she hated them.

She had a lot to think about. She had not intended to get into a fight. Maybe streaks in families came like a streak of lightning. It had hit her and caused her to fight.

Her problem now was to get upstairs before Nana saw her torn dress and tearstained face. Fortunately, Nana was sewing at the dining-room table with her back to the door when Catherine came home.

At the top of the stairs, Catherine looked down through the archway into the dining room. Beside the machine and scattered on the floor around Nana were pieces of white cloth with big orange spots. It was the ugliest fabric Catherine had ever seen. "Are you making me a dress out of that?" she shrieked.

"Why, no, hon, I got out this old Simplicity pattern, and I'm making you a clown suit for Halloween. I wish now I hadn't given that other one I made a long time ago to the rummage."

"I'm not going to the school party, and I'm not going to trick or treat either. I don't need that thing," Catherine yelled.

"My, what's got into you?" Nana carefully placed fabric under the needle. "This is a nice suit. You'd be surprised how much work there is to one of these."

Catherine tore the armhole of her dress even more as she yanked it off in her room. Here she'd had about the worst day possible, and Nana was down there yammering about a stupid clown suit. She got into her after-school jeans and shirt.

Now where was that mending kit Nana was always reminding her of? She gave the dressing-table drawer a hard pull, and it came all the way out. The contents scattered over the floor.

Catherine picked everything up and spent a long time carefully mending her dress. The work made her feel fit to go downstairs and get through Nana's boiled dinner, although she didn't eat much. Boiling was about the worst thing that could be done to a dinner.

She went to sleep easily enough later, but she woke often and couldn't make sense of her strange dreams. In one, she hit Mr. Beaumont right in the stomach. Something broke in there, and he couldn't get his breath. Then they both had to talk to the elementary counselor, who was wearing a clown suit, white with big orange dots.

6

It was very early in the morning when Catherine shook off her dreams and awoke. She wished it were Saturday. The kids at school might forget about the fight over a weekend. But it was Thursday.

She got out of bed, turned on the light, and stared at herself in the dressing-table mirror. She thought she looked kind of sick. Maybe if she could look sicker, Nana would let her stay home from school for a couple of days. But then Miss Kneehoff might telephone, wanting to know what was wrong. If Nana talked to anybody at school, they'd probably tell her about the fight. The best thing to do was go on to school and act as if nothing had happened.

The first person Catherine saw at the school entrance was Bryan Jones. "Hi, Ali," he said, and pulled up the leg of his jeans to show a black-and-blue bruise.

Scott Norton came over and pointed to a bruise on his arm. "Mine's yellow, kind of like chicken skin. Ali really popped me one, and I didn't do nothing to her."

Ali! That's what they were going to call her. She'd wanted a nickname—something cute like Bobbi—but now she knew she was stuck with Ali. Mr. Beaumont didn't say a word about the fight, but he, too, was calling her Ali by late afternoon.

The next two days she walked home from school alone as fast as she could. On the third day, Bobbi and Diane ran to catch up with her. "Ali, I'm sorry," Bobbi said, panting. "Afterward I felt crummy about yelling like the others when I live in the same block. I don't know why I did it."

"I'm sorry, Ali," Diane announced. "My mother told me I was to apologize to you. She said, 'There but for the grace of God, goes my child.'"

"What's that supposed to mean?" Ali asked.

"I don't know, but just remember, Ali, I was supposed to say I'm sorry, and I said it."

"Did you tell Nana you started a fight and punched a lot of kids?" Bobbi asked. "Did she see where your dress was torn?"

"No, I didn't tell her, and you better not either. I sewed up my dress myself and put it in the wash.

It's permanent press and won't need ironing, so she won't even notice the mend. She and Pop won't ever know what happened."

She thought she could be right. If Nana asked why Mr. Beaumont and the kids called her Ali, she'd just say because they wanted to. But she knew something was different the day before Halloween. Pop asked her to come help him in the shop. He'd never done that before; usually she just followed him out there.

She helped spread newspapers over his workbench. "Now what are we going to do?"

"First, Nana says I've got to talk to you about school. Says its my turn. Claims if she tried to talk to you it wouldn't be a whipstitch before she's crying and you're yelling."

"Wouldn't either. Nothing going on at school except a Halloween party tomorrow. I made a batch of brownies from a mix. I was going to make them from scratch, but I'm tired of hearing about that dumb party. That's all they talk about at school."

"I hear they were talking about something else too—a regular Donnybrook," Pop said.

Donnybrook sounded like the name of some store bread or maybe a gift shop. "What's that?"

"A fight. Nana and I heard you were in the thick of it."

"Who told you?"

"Henrietta."

"Henrietta! Do you know Miss Kneehoff well enough to call her by her first name?"

"Sure. I remember when I used to give her red pigtails a yank. Now she's principal and has to let folks know what goes on at school. She uses a lot of big words now. Aggressive behavior, she called it. Sounded to me like you knocked them into the middle of next week. How did you come to do that?"

"I didn't *come* to do it. What they were yelling got me so mad that I started to hit and kick and pull and maybe even bite." Ali flung her arms about and kicked to demonstrate.

"Beat the daylights out of them." Pop shook his head. "Very aggressive behavior, Catherine."

"You might as well call me Ali. That's what they call me now at school. Mr. Beaumont started it. I wanted a cute nickname."

"Which would you rather be—tough or cute?"

Ali straightened her shoulders. "Tough, I guess. I'm too tall to be cute."

"Are you still mad at the kids?"

"Not quite. They let me know about my mother. Now I know what kind of sick it is. Maybe I should put a gold star on everybody's forehead the way

Miss Kneehoff used to do in second grade." Ali's voice dropped. "They told me more than you and Nana did. I ought to be sore at you."

"I always dreaded you'd hear it the way you did." Pop shook his head. "I'm glad you gave them a few blows. I wanted to tell you, but Nana didn't think we should put worries in your young life until you were—"

"I know, until I was old enough to understand. I'm old enough, and I want to know why my mother landed in the hospital."

Pop took his knife from his pocket, opened a blade, and began to sharpen it on his whetstone. "If I could tell you just exactly why that happened, I'd be smarter than the doctors. It's hard to know why it happened, why it happened to her and to us. Some things you just have to accept."

"You talk like it's going to be forever."

"I've seen more things happen—and not happen —than you have. Why, when I was a young fellow, I thought I could do anything. In no time, I was an old fellow and knew it wasn't true. So my other worry was that you would suffer most when you finally had to accept that some things can't be changed. I wasn't sure you could realize that."

"Pop, you just stop talking that way!" Ali beat at his arms with clenched fists. "Stop it!"

"All right, all right. Simmer down, Ali. I'll tell

you something. I was supposed to rake you over the coals, but I'm kind of proud of you. Before I got my growth, I was a puny kid, always getting beat up. That's what kids in my grade did for amusement—beat up on Thurman McNair. I decided that if I ever met a kid I could whip, I'd whip him every day."

Ali couldn't help but laugh a little over such a silly ambition.

"A fighter has to know when to go to a neutral corner," Pop said. "We can't think about this trouble all the time. Best put what minds we have on something else for a while. We'll give the kids at school something else to think about too."

Pop pulled a bushel basket of pumpkins out from under his workbench. "You remember we planted punkin seeds and gourd seeds last summer?"

"On the bank out back of the shop. Yes, but I forgot about them. I didn't go back there all summer long. I didn't weed them or anything. I forgot."

"You forgot, and so did I, but the bees didn't. We have a crop of mighty strange-looking punkins. Look here." Pop pointed to odd clusters of bumps on the pumpkins.

"What happened to them?" Ali ran her hand over the bumps.

"Near as I can tell, the punkins and the gourds got mixed up," Pop said. "We planted some warty gourds to vine out and cover the bank. Bees cross-pollinated them with the punkins. Now I was thinking we could make some unusual jack-o'-lanterns out of a couple of them."

"Sure, warts and all." She inspected the pumpkins. "Here's one with lots of warts in the right places. Can I use your knife?"

Ali made two jack-o'-lanterns for school and an extra one for home. Pop was talked out, but they worked so late that Nana had to come out and tell Ali it was bedtime. Nana smiled when she saw the jack-o'-lanterns. She said one with a turned-down mouth reminded her of her cousin Delbert, Ted's brother.

The next morning Ali carried a jack-o'-lantern under each arm to school. Mr. Beaumont set them on his desk and stood back to get a good look. "I've seen lots of pumpkins—little ones, big ones, green, lopsided—but these are pumpkins with knobs on them."

Scott Norton examined the bumps. "You must have planted some special seed. What was it, Ali?"

"No, nothing special in the seed."

"Must be a mutation," Scott speculated. "Better keep the seed."

"Gives that jack-o' real character," Mr. Beaumont said.

The class gathered round. "Look at them," someone commented. "Dig those craa— those funny-looking things."

Ali noticed the word change. A few days ago they were shouting cruddy stuff at her. Now they were careful not to use the word *crazy*. It was some improvement but still not right.

"Now class, we have a lot to do in the AM," Mr. Beaumont said, "for we have a big PM coming up." He looked at the jack-o'-lanterns and at Ali. "Some pumpkins, some pumpkins."

Ali decided to enjoy the party, and she did. Just like Pop said. You couldn't think of your troubles all the time.

After the parade around the neighborhood, costume judging, and refreshments, Ali was glad to get out of her clown suit and walk in the bright autumn sunshine. Bobbi still wore her Snoopy suit but carried its head. "And another good thing about today, Ali, you were supposed to see Ms. Rosengren, but she didn't show due to Halloween."

Ali sighed. "I have to see her at least once more, I guess. That's what she told me—well, after that fight."

"Did she yell at you?"

"Nope. She said I had helped her by expressing myself overtly in gross motor activity. That gave her some input for recommendations, so perhaps one more counseling session might be sufficient."

"How can you remember all that stuff?"

"I looked up the words I didn't know in Big Web."

Clack, clack. Diane wobbled up on high heels. She was supposed to be Cher and wore a long, black wig. "Ali, I don't blame you for taking off your clown suit," Diane said. "I had one in kindergarten. My little brother Jonathan wouldn't even wear it this year."

"You'll break your neck in those heels," Ali said.

Diane tossed her long, black locks. "Won't either. Even if you're tall, you'll have to learn to walk in them, same as every other girl."

"It's one thing I'm going to skip," Ali said.

7

Ms. Rosengren was shuffling file folders, trying to locate the D's when Ali came into the little room off the nurse's office.

Ali handed her a sheet of paper. "This is that autobiography, the one you said you'd be flexible about when school started. I finally got it done."

Ms. Rosengren nodded and read:

Catherine "Ali" Doyle, grade 5, age 10. I live with my grandparents, Thurman and Betty McNair. I have no brothers or sisters. I have always lived in St. Stephen. There are 10,000 people in St. Stephen, and almost all of them always lived here. When I was 6, I had a dog named Gyp. I like to read.

❊   ❊   ❊

"Is this all?" Ms. Rosengren was amazed.

" 'Tis for now."

"You could include your evaluation of the attitudes of your classmates, how they have affected you. Don't you wish to do so? You have time now."

Ali thought about the kids in fifth grade. Mean as some of them were, they'd been her classmates since kindergarten. Bryan Jones might turn out to be some kind of second-rate genius. Eric Huskey might stumble onto a wad of money while pawing through junk. It was better to walk home with Bobbi and even old Diane than to walk alone. Her ideas didn't seem to add up to an evaluation. She shook her head and slid the sheet of paper back across the table to Ms. Rosengren.

"Very well, Ali. I'll mark that a self-initiated motivation to complete a project. That's commendable. I'll put it in your folder. Now since you've done this for me before your conference, you may go back to your classroom. I have a number of profiles to do and can use the time."

Skipping wasn't allowed in the hall, but Ali felt so good she risked a few skips anyhow.

Several days later she wondered if they had heard at home about her self-initiated motivation. After Pop had watched the weather show on TV, she followed him into his shop.

"We might as well leave Nana's curtain over the glass," Pop said. "Days are so short now that we'll have to turn on all our lights."

"Have you had any more calls from your old school chum, Henrietta Kneehoff?"

"Not a peep." Pop pulled the chains of two bulbs. "Should I? Have you been in another fracas?"

"Not me!"

"I didn't think so. Nana said you've been so good lately that butter wouldn't melt in your mouth. Is that because it's nearer Christmas?"

"Do you remember what I told you about Christmas this year? All I want is to see my mother."

"And I said you'd change your mind by the time snow flies. None yet and none coming for a while, according to the weather show."

"Pop, what color are my mother's eyes?"

"Right out of the blue."

"You mean sky blue, like the summer sky?"

"No. That question, Ali, so unexpected. Right out of the clear blue sky, as they say."

"Well, what color are they?"

"That would be right, like the summer sky."

"I want to see for myself. You said she could have visitors. Does my father go to see her?"

Pop took a hammer from his toolbox. "No, not him."

"He doesn't come to see me either. I guess he's dead, and you don't want to tell me until I'm old enough to understand. I've known about dead ever since Gyp got run over a long time ago."

"I didn't say he was dead, Ali."

There it was again. Ali felt that scared, sick feeling. She was thankful that Pop plugged in his electric drill and there was too much noise to talk. She really didn't want to know for certain that her father had just gone away. Once she'd said so for a joke, trying to shock Nana; but now it seemed too possible, too real.

She ran from the shop across the dark yard into the house. In her room, she sat for a few minutes at the dressing table. Then she went to the closet and stood on tiptoe trying to reach the big books on the shelf.

A little perfume bottle fell from the shelf to her feet. It didn't break. Ali picked it up, took out the stopper, and smelled the few remaining drops. Mysteriously, the scared feeling went away, and she was calmer.

She studied the worn label on the bottle. It must have been her mother's perfume. How could Nana have overlooked it?

Every spring Nana went through the house, tossing things into boxes for the church rummage sale. Before Ali and Pop could rescue anything, she loaded the boxes into the old Chevy and drove off to the church. She must have thought the bottle was too empty for rummage and too full for trash.

Ali brought the dressing-table chair over to the closet. She wanted to make sure there was nothing else on the shelf besides the three yearbooks from St. Stephen High School. She replaced the perfume bottle in a far corner; then she took down the books entitled *The Excelsior* one by one.

The yearbook name sounded the same as the shredded-wood packing material in Pop's shop. She'd have to look up that word in Big Web.

As she often did, Ali studied the pictures of the boys. Their hair was cut close to their heads. Most of them must have gone directly from the barbershop to the photographer. Ali had searched many times for a boy with her last name. The only Doyle was an ugly girl.

She knew the page with her mother's picture in each book. With each passing high-school year, the pictures got bigger, and her mother got prettier. "Still water runs deep" was printed beside Kathleen McNair's senior picture. The face that gazed out at Ali was both mysterious and familiar. After much study, Ali had decided that her mother looked like Pop, although she couldn't determine exactly how a young girl could look like a man who would get his Social Security in two years. Perhaps it was the set of the mouth or the look from the grave eyes. Now she knew they were sky blue. Kathleen's hair seemed to be dark brown, like Ali's.

Ali pored over photographs of teachers, athletic teams, play casts, and future secretaries. She wondered if the Glee Club was expected to be gleeful at all times.

Kathleen McNair was in the front row of a group picture of the Palette and Brush Club. All the girls wore skirts. Kathleen's was plaid. Her white blouse outlined the neck of her cardigan. She wore white sneakers. Her hair was cut short, puffed out at the side, with little wispy bangs on her forehead.

Classmates had written all over the pages of the books. "Cathy, never forget P and B Club and econ," was signed "Bruce." Beth L. dotted the *i*'s of her note with circles.

After looking at all the pictures of her mother and reading the notes from her classmates, Ali felt reassured. Her mother was just as real as Bobbi's mother, and her father was somewhere, if not in that book.

Carefully she put the *Excelsiors* back on the shelf. She thought of the snapshots downstairs in the table drawer. Nana called it a library table, although it was in the living room and not in a library. Those snapshots might help solve the puzzle of how a young girl could look like Pop.

Nana was cooking spaghetti sauce and didn't notice Ali slip into the living room. She took out the albums, half-filled with faded black-and-white snapshots of a young man and woman who looked oddly like Pop and Nana. A different album had baby pictures and photographs of a little girl with long curls. She wore ruffled dresses, and it was always summer.

Ali had just started to look at the pictures still in the photographer's yellow envelopes when Nana came into the living room. "Are you into those things again?" The frown wrinkle was deep between Nana's eyes. "Don't drag them out. Let bygones be bygones. Don't ask me about them. It's too much to put a person through. Hurts for no reason."

"But, Nana, I want to. . . ."

"Put them back. Shut, oh, shut the drawer. Leave it alone. Go set the table."

After supper Ali went to the library table to get the *St. Stephen Sentinel* for Pop. She pulled on the drawer. It was locked.

8

Nana's locking a drawer like that, just as if she were a baby, trying to poison herself or something, was insulting. Nana could be an awful pain sometimes. Ali wanted to tell her off. But, like as not, Nana wouldn't even listen. She was beginning to go around in circles, muttering that Christmas was upon her.

At school, Mr. Beaumont was casual about Christmas, but Miss Kneehoff seemed to think it called for riot control. She came into their classroom and announced that they were to remain calm. They would make some simple decorations for the classroom, handcraft gifts for parents, take part in the school assembly. That would be all! The way she said *all* didn't sound very calm.

Mr. Beaumont let them vote on what to make. Plastic-lined makeup bags for mothers and tie racks for fathers won. Ali thought both were super corny.

"I've got mine done, all gift wrapped and everything," Bobbi announced to Ali and Diane, as they walked up the hill from school on a chilly, windy day.

"What's the hurry?" Ali asked. "It's still quite a while before Christmas."

"I'll have mine done by Friday," Diane said.

"Pop doesn't wear a necktie unless somebody dies and he goes to the funeral home," Ali said. "Nana wouldn't want a tie rack cluttering things up. She'd give it to the church rummage."

"It would be a present anyhow," Diane reminded her.

"And a makeup bag wouldn't do Nana any good," Ali continued. "She doesn't paint her eyelids blue or anything."

"She could put her toothbrush in it or her denture cream. I guess she has false teeth." Diane giggled.

"She does not!" Ali stated firmly. "She's told me why often enough. When she was a kid, she had hardly any candy and pop. She only had ice cream once a year, on the Fourth of July."

They came to Bobbi's front walk. "Want to come in and see if we can make some hot chocolate?"

Bobbi opened the front door to a rush of warm air, the aroma of coffee, and a chatter of voices.

"It's Wednesday! Sunshine Circle! My mother doesn't take any hair appointments. Come on, there ought to be cookies," she said, excited.

Bobbi led the way to the dining room, where her mother, Diane's mother, and four other women worked at the table piled with Christmas wrapping paper, stacks of notepaper, soap, razor blades, wallets, paperback books, panty hose, ball-point pens, and other stuff. The place looked like the C and B Cut-Rate.

"Hi, girls," Mrs. Clark greeted them. "I guess all you ladies know my girl, Bobbi; Fran's girl, Diane; and their friend, Ali."

A round-faced woman with short gray hair gazed at them over the top of her glasses. "Oh, yes, Bobbi looks just for the world like her dad. You named her right. I'd know Fran's daughter anywhere, and, of course, Catherine McNair."

"My name's Doyle, Ali Doyle."

"Yes, yes, but I think of it as McNair, same as your grandmother." She sighed and clicked her tongue.

"There are some cookies in the kitchen, girls. Bobbi, you can make some instant cocoa," Mrs. Clark said.

"Now just a minute," cried a skinny lady with a shrill voice. "Just a little old minute before we get into that cookie routine. How about some gift wrapping, girls? We might as well use these young hands." She pushed paper, scissors, and a can of shaving cream toward Ali. "Now where's that extra roll of Scotch tape?"

Ali cut a piece of holly paper the right size to wrap around a can. "What's all this for?"

"What's it for?" The woman shrieked in surprise. "Don't you tell these girls about our sunshine projects, Sue? These are gifts for people who would, like as not, be forgotten at Christmas, for people at the Webbs Flats State Hospital. They—"

"Mercy, mercy," interrupted a tiny old lady with a voice deep as Pop's. "It's snowing!" She got up and tottered to the window. "I declare, the first snow of the year."

Ali thought she was making quite a fuss over a few snowflakes, but maybe that's the way it was with ladies even older than Nana.

"Oh, I hate to see the snow come," Diane's mother moaned. "We are sunshine-circle girls, not snow elves."

The gray-haired lady wrapped a package of pink-plastic hair rollers. "Best get this job done then and deliver these gifts to the state hospital before we get a big storm and bad roads."

"Yes, indeed." The skinny woman whacked off a length of paper. "I can't spend too much time on this, not when there's so much to do this time of year. Finish wrapping and take this stuff over to Webbs Flats right away. It won't matter if it comes early. Most of them wouldn't know the difference anyhow. You know, they pamper them now. They don't have to do a hand's turn unless they get paid —paid, mind you—for what little or nothing they would be able. . . ."

"Bobbi, go get your cookies," Mrs. Clark ordered.

The gray-haired woman stared over the top of her glasses at Ali. "It's so sad," she murmured.

As they went to the kitchen, Ali heard Diane's mother say, "There but for the grace of God, my girl could go."

Ali felt gripped by anger. "I don't want any cookies, Bobbi," she said, and ran outside, slamming the back door as she left.

If only she could hit something or somebody, the way she had when she got her nickname. She'd like to go back and sweep the entire sunshine project off the table onto the floor. That would make old skin-and-bones yell. She raced past her own house, relieved to be outside with snow whirling around her. But maybe if she had hit somebody, Diane's mother would begin to yammer about streaks in families.

By the time she retraced her tracks home, she felt better. It was dumb not to grab some of those fancy Christmas cookies.

If they were to have any at home, she'd have to bake them herself. Nana was too busy sewing. Ali heard the machine whirring when she came in. Nana had cut up an old green garment and was making it over into some kind of big coat. It was awful ugly.

Without looking up from the purple braid she was sewing on, Nana said, "Are your feet wet? Might as well get your boots out. I sure hope you haven't outgrown them. You'll need them from now on. We're in for it."

"That's too big for me. Who's it for?" Ali asked.

"Never mind."

"Pop won't like it. Is it for him?"

"I said 'never mind.'"

"You should have given that green thing to the rummage."

Nana put down her scissors with a clatter. "Now look here, that's enough of your aggravating. Just about enough. Go set the table."

"I won't do it," Ali blurted out.

"What!" Nana looked up in astonishment.

Ali fled upstairs. Nana didn't climb steps unless she had to.

"What did you say?" Nana stood, hands on hips, at the bottom of the stairs. "Did I hear what I think I heard?"

"You did if you're not deaf," Ali mumbled.

"'How sharper than a serpent's tooth it is to have a thankless child,'" Nana called up the stairs.

Now what was that supposed to mean? Was she some kind of a snake because she didn't want Nana to get all tired out and crabby making somebody that slime-green thing with purple braid?

Then a dreadful thought occured to her. Nana was making a Christmas robe for her mother. Still water runs deep. Her mother would take that hideous robe, look at it gravely, and not say she disliked it. Then she would get a fancy package of pink-plastic hair rollers from the Sunshine Circle. That would be Christmas.

Ali kept her money in the top drawer of the dressing table in a change purse shaped like a Scot's tam. She had bought it when they went to Niagara Falls, Canada, with Cousin Ted. The tam was bulging. She emptied its contents on her bed and counted out $7.84, which was good considering she was unemployed.

She replaced the tam and looked out her window at the falling snow. Pop had come home and started a fire in the shop. Smoke blew from the tin chimney toward the ground. Pop said smoke drifting down meant more snow.

Downstairs, Nana rattled dishes. Ali slipped down the steps and out the front door to avoid the kitchen.

She went around the house, across the yard, and into the shop.

Snow had come over the tops of her shoes, so she took them off and held her feet near the stove.

Pop sanded a tabletop. "How are you and Nana getting along?"

"Okay."

"Not according to her. She claims you were disobedient and impudent."

"I was disobedient, anyhow. I don't know about impudent. What's that?"

"I don't know exactly myself, but it's something you should not be toward a person like Nana, who works hard and does good ninety percent of the time."

"Some do-good people make me awful mad," Ali confided.

"Yes, I know, but we've got to put up with them."

"Nana was hollering about a serpent's tooth," Ali said.

Pop smiled. "All this time, Betty has remembered her Shakespeare. I'm not surprised. She was the smartest one in our class. Maybe that's when I began to believe whatever Betty said must be the case. In our last year of high school, we had this English teacher who made us learn some Shakespeare by heart."

Ali tried to imagine Nana and Pop in high school, looking the way they did in the old snapshot album. Pop stood straight and slender. Nana, in dresses almost to her ankles, had no frown line at all.

"You might be surprised to know I remember some Shakespeare myself." Pop pushed back the curtain on the glass door. Snow blew aslant. "'Blow, blow thou winter wind, Thou are not so unkind as man's ingratitude.'"

"Pop, that Shakespeare is awful heavy. Do you think I'm worse than a biting snake and downright ungrateful?"

"Not on your life, Ali. If I thought so, I wouldn't say it in Shakespeare. I'd come right out in English. You're just a little bullheaded at times."

"Yes, I guess so, maybe. The snow is flying, Pop. Remember what you said? I haven't changed my mind about what I want this Christmas. I still want to see my mother. Now I have a special reason. More than ever I want to see her. I'm real bullheaded about it."

9

Pop was turning the old Chevy into the driveway as Ali came home from school. Together they went into the kitchen, which was cluttered with gommed-up mixing bowls, baking pans, and crumpled foil. Nana didn't look very neat, either.

Pop sniffed the spicy air. "Smells mighty good. What's for supper?"

"Supper! Oh, Lord, I don't know. I've spent the whole day making fruitcakes. I should have gotten at it sooner. They're better if they age. I didn't think about supper. I'll scare up something. It's three meals a day, Christmas or no Christmas."

"Bobbi's mother does all that, and she works to make money, too," Ali said.

"Well, I guess Sue Clark is a superwoman." Nana sniffed. "I'm not. Besides, she's younger than I am."

DENVER
PUBLIC · · ARY

SEP '80

CITY & COUNTY OF DENVER

Ali counted the cooling fruitcakes. "Who are they for?"

"For Cousin Delbert. One's for Cousin Ted. I couldn't forget him."

"He doesn't need it."

"It's near Christmas, Catherine. Now set the table."

"Nana, why don't you call me Ali, the same as everybody else does?"

"That would be hard for me to do."

"You could think of me as Catherine and call me Ali for short. Bryan Jones says if you keep calling me Catherine, I might get an identity crisis."

"What's that?" Nana asked.

"Oh, I don't know. Something that's going around."

"Well, I'll try. Now set the table."

"I can't, Nana. I have to go to the library and get something on Christmas-in-many-lands. It's for the report my group voted to have. I want to be ready when I'm called on," Ali said.

"Now look here, Ali, don't get loaded down with books and expect us to come get you. It's going to snow again. Streets will be icy. Pop's tired after a shift of work, and I've got more cakes in the oven."

As Ali went into the library, Bryan Jones came

out with an armful of books and climbed into his mother's waiting car. When Ali checked the shelves, she found no books on Christmas-in-many-lands. Bryan had got there first and hogged everything again.

She had said she was going to the library, and so she had. Ali headed across the new city parking lot toward Christopher's, the biggest store in St. Stephen.

Clerks in the sportswear department were so busy that she herself located a blue, knit turtleneck blouse on the rack. Nana didn't like that style. She said it didn't look good on anything but a turtle. Ali visualized her mother's face as it was in the *Excelsior* and decided the blue top was the right style. The color was right, too.

She read the price ticket and the label, which stated the garment was 100 percent acrylic. She liked the washing instructions: toss into washer, toss into dryer.

An elderly clerk, whose feet seemed to hurt with every step, swayed up to her. "Now I see you've picked the nicest color in these knits that we have, and they are a special price, too. What size?"

"This, I guess." Ali took the blouse from the rack.

"That's small. I think your grandmother would take a large."

Ali didn't recognize the clerk, but perhaps the woman remembered seeing Ali and Nana in the store together. Maybe she was in Nana's church circle. Having someone she didn't even recognize know her grandmother's size was creepy. Ali thought of her mother's slender face in the pictures. She insisted on the small size.

Lurching from side to side on her swollen feet, the clerk went to the counter. "Will this be cash or charge?"

"Cash." Ali counted money from her tam purse.

"Are you sure you don't want large, or at least medium?"

Ali nodded. She wished she knew all the people who seemed to know her. The clerk folded the blouse to fit into a flimsy gift box and put it into a huge paper bag.

As she pushed hard on the big door and went out into the cold, Ali had a sinking feeling. The picture in the *Excelsior* was taken long ago. The blouse might be too small. Maybe her mother couldn't wear a blue, knit, 100 percent acrylic, $6.75 turtleneck blouse at all. She was in the hospital; she was sick. Maybe she wore a nightgown all the time. Nana had made her a robe.

Ali hadn't been in Christopher's for long, but it was dark and snowing when she left. Once she got away from the lights of store windows and of downtown traffic, it seemed like the middle of the night.

She had eight blocks to go. The first part of the way was along Main, past the biggest houses in St. Stephen. Rich people still lived in some of them. Others had been converted into funeral homes or apartments. Nana knew who was rich in St. Stephen. She even knew who had been rich and wasn't anymore.

Ali turned toward the park. It was darker than ever. She started to run, and the big bag hit against her legs. She'd have trouble getting it upstairs and hidden in her room without Nana seeing it. A TV special she'd seen showed how whole forests were cut down to make big bags nobody needed. She considered carrying the box and throwing away the bag, but that would be littering, something that could land a person in jail.

A familiar, cheerful ring sounded. A chain from a playground swing clanged against the swing support. It reminded her of long summer evenings when she had played in the park. If it were summer, there would be broad daylight for hours yet. So what was scary about five o'clock, even in December?

Ali trudged on, up the steep hill. The street was lined with narrow, two-storied, gabled houses built by Nana's busy contractor.

Nana opened the front door. "It's pitch dark. I

was getting anxious about you. No books, and a parcel from Christopher's? Well, I won't be nosey this time of year, just in case it's for me. You can leave it right here on the telephone table. Come set the table. I've got a path cleared in the kitchen."

When Ali had hung up her coat, she went into the kitchen to help. "What happened to those books you needed?" Nana asked.

"Bryan Jones got to them first," Ali said, as she took plates from the cabinet. "I guess he needs them too. He's got that big IQ and has to keep it fired up. I don't know what my IQ is. Mr. Beaumont wouldn't tell me, but he might tell you, Nana, if you asked him."

"I don't believe in IQ," Nana said, dishing up scrambled eggs. She'd made home fries and cole slaw too.

"For a while there, I thought we were going to have chopped-up dates and orange peel for supper," Pop said as he sat down at the table. "That's all I saw in the kitchen."

"I hate that stuff," Ali said. "It tastes like varnish."

"You had a mess of varnish lately?" Pop asked.

Nana passed around dessert dishes of canned peaches. "Dried fruit, raisins, suet, spice, nuts, and all that goes back to when people didn't have everything in this wide world all times of the year. Fruit in winter was something special. It was dried and saved for holiday cakes and puddings."

After supper Nana announced that she was all in but the shoestrings. Pop put on her apron and washed dishes. As Ali dried, the thought of the beautiful blue blouse made her feel happy. Soon they were finished and she took her parcel along when she went upstairs.

Ali still had to try to think of something for verbal arts. Suddenly she remembered what Nana had told them at supper. That might do. She began to write.

One thing people do in many lands at Christmas is make fruitcakes, which also have got nuts. It goes way back to when there wasn't any fresh fruit in winter. So the fruit was dried. They never stopped doing this, and in many lands they use dates, raisins. . . .

"Nana," Ali called downstairs. "What's that stuff tastes like varnish in fruitcake?"

"Citron," Nana called back.

Ali stopped to admire the blouse, then continued to write.

. . . citron, and spice which had got discovered. They made puddings out of suet, which is what is usually fed to birds in winter nowadays when people have everything in this wide world.

That should be enough. She had time still for a final look at the blouse. It was so soft. A person could wear it even in bed. Ali fastened the lid down with Scotch tape and put the box far back in her closet. If something was all done up like that, Nana wouldn't open it and waste the tape.

She went to bed early but stayed awake, thinking of how long it was from one Christmas to another. She remembered that both Pop and Nana always went somewhere for a whole day in early December. Last year Nana had said they had Christmas work to do. Ali supposed they'd gone shopping. Now she realized Pop would not go in and out of stores all day long.

They took a day before Christmas to go to Webbs Flats and see her mother in the hospital. This year would be different. She was going, too.

10

At school the next day, Ali didn't worry that her report was homemade. She was sure it would be better than most of them. Eric Huskey jazzed his up with a lot of gadgets, which he claimed came from many lands. Ali raised her hand. Might as well get it over with.

She read her first sentence with confidence and looked up at the class. There was a smirk on Diane's face. She was sure of it. Silently she reread the sentence and realized what was wrong. No one had taunted her for a long time. If she went on with her fruitcake report, Diane or someone was bound to come up with—nutty as a fruitcake. She'd better not risk it.

Ali turned to Mr. Beaumont. "I don't have mine finished."

He glanced at her paper. "Don't I detect more? That's not your common copied-from-the-encyclopedia report. We'd be glad to hear it."

"The books were all out. Somebody checked them all out." Ali went to her seat. She wanted to slump down, for she felt a wave of the same sickening fear that had overwhelmed her on the day Diane let her know about her mother's illness. Sometimes, when she least expected it, there was that awful feeling of being afraid and mad at the same time. She straightened up in her seat. Nobody was going to get her that scared and angry again, not when she had plans to think about.

Mr. Beaumont didn't write anything in his book, but then he usually didn't. He kept things in his head—things like an unfinished gift project, an unprepared assignment. Ali wondered if he passed these failures on to Miss Kneehoff or, worse, to Ms. Rosengren. At school, she wasn't doing so well on Christmas.

She was beginning to have other doubts about the holiday, too. Maybe the blouse was too small. Her mother might be as fat as Cousin Ted from all that time in the hospital.

The school week finally ended. On Friday night Ali took the *Excelsiors* down from the shelf. Carefully she studied the pictures of her mother in each book. Kathleen McNair looked mild and calm, as if butter wouldn't melt in her mouth, as Nana would say. There was no hint of what was to come.

All at once, Ali felt very weary. She had only this paper mother, not a real, live, flesh-and-blood mother like other kids. Why had she let herself get sick and stay sick? Ali slammed the book shut. Nana was right. It was best to shut the books the way she had shut the library table drawer.

At breakfast next morning Nana announced, "You're to stay at Clarks' today, Ali. They expect you. Pop and I won't be home."

Ali felt her stomach tighten. Maybe she should stay at Clarks' instead of getting Nana all upset. But she'd made her plans and was going to stick with them. "I'm not staying a whole day with Bobbi. She's mean when she gets a chance," Ali declared.

"Yes, you are. We're taking a day off. People are allowed to do that this time of year. You and Bobbi ought to have a good day. Sue Clark will be busy doing hair for holiday parties, so don't hinder her."

Ali ran upstairs and came down with her package. She took her ski jacket and knit cap from the rack by the front door. "I'm going with you."

Nana groaned as she bent over to put on her shoe boots. "We'll see about that."

Ali's heart pounded as she got into the Chevy. Nana came out with a large gift-wrapped package and three smaller ones. As she opened the car door,

77

she saw Ali in the back seat. "I declare, if you were a little pet dog, I'd drag you right out of there. But you're a big girl, and you ought to behave like one."

Pop got in the driver's seat and started the motor. "Leave her off at Clarks'," Nana said to him.

Pop picked up speed as he drove past Clarks'. Ali's heart picked up speed, too.

"Thurman!" Nana yelled. "I told you, stop at Clarks'. You're getting more absentminded every day."

Pop kept on going downhill. "Ali might as well ride over to Webbs Flats with us."

"I wish I had my hands on that steering wheel and my foot on that brake," Nana said, fuming.

They drove down River Street past the Castex plant, where Pop raised his hand to some workmen standing by an entrance. River Street soon turned into Route 86. There was a cluster of low new houses with big lawns off the highway. Nana could hardly keep track of the rich people who didn't used to be rich living there.

Ali watched for her special willow tree on the bank of the St. Stephen River. She felt that she owned that tree because she noticed it every time she passed. Last time it had been trimmed with a narrow gold leaves. Today none were left.

Route 86 followed the valley of the river, which

looked as cold and gray as the sky it reflected. The bordering hills were gray-purple with a fringe of trees on top.

Slices of plowed snow melted on the berm of the highway, wet and bare from a sprinkling of salt. The salt made driving in winter easier, but it killed the trees near the road and rusted the old Chevy. Lots of things seemed to be both good and bad.

Pop needed no help with navigation. He knew every turn. As usual, he was quiet, but Ali thought maybe he had some plan. Nana didn't say anything for the first hour. When Pop turned on the radio and some dogs began to bark "Jingle Bells," Nana turned it off. She said singing dogs made her nervous.

There were no plants or factories at the edge of Webbs Flats. All at once, they were in the center of the little town. A sign pointed toward the hospital. They were still in New York State, still in the Chevy, but Ali felt as excited as if she were about to enter a star world.

The hospital was a cluster of buildings on an open, snowy tract. They didn't match. Low redbrick ones looked new. The old buildings were stone, gray as the winter sky. Pop drove toward an old one with four towers.

Ali had seen similar castles on book jackets. A

young woman with long hair and her cape flowing in the wind should have been running away. Instead, people were going in.

Pop found a parking place near the stone steps of the entrance. Nana picked up her large package and one small one. "You'll have a long cold wait out here, Ali."

"I'm coming, too."

Nana gasped. "Now you look here, Ali. You don't know what you're talking about. You can't come barging into this hospital. We'd have to discuss that with Mr. What's His Name."

"Mr. Pienkowski," Pop recalled.

"Who's that?"

"The social worker," Nana explained. "He knows what people ought to do, talks to people."

"I'm going in to see my mother."

"Oh, no! You can't do that without some preparation. Kathleen would need to know you were coming. You marching in would be a shock. Wouldn't it, Thurman?"

"She's here. Might as well let her come in with us."

"It could give Kathleen an awful backset," Nana asserted.

"Might perk her up," Pop speculated.

"You're on Ali's side, just the way you were on

Kathleen's. I did everything for that girl, and then *he* came along." Nana was growing more upset as she talked.

"Who's he?" Ali didn't expect an answer.

"Mark Doyle, that's who!" Nana surprised her. "Your mother drove her ducks to a poor market when she fell for that one. She climbed Fool's Hill. I told her and told her, over and over again, but she wouldn't listen, wouldn't give us a second thought. You know it, Thurman. I blame him, and I blame myself." Nana began to cry.

Pop put his arm around her. "Don't blame yourself or blame anybody. Things happen in this life."

"It's a vale of tears," Nana cried. "Now you tell me, Thurman. What have we done to be tortured like this? I just try and try my level best and always have." Nana sobbed and talked at the same time. She sounded awful and looked worse.

Ali was sure that people passing were staring at them. "I want to go in. I'm not staying out here in the cold any longer."

"I always try to muster up a little happiness when Christmas is coming. Now Ali will spoil Christmas for all of us," Nana said, sobbing.

"I'm right here. Why are you talking as if I wasn't here?" Ali demanded.

Nana blew her nose. "I can't go in to see Kathleen

when I'm all worked up like this. Let's walk around the grounds a bit until I feel more like a human being, Thurman."

Pop helped Nana out of the car. Ali sat far back in the seat so that no one passing would connect her with that stoop-shouldered man and crybaby old woman.

She watched them go down the drive, walking as if they were one hundred years old. Some people might think they were a nice old couple. She knew they were not! Nana had sat right there in the front seat of the Chevy and said Ali would try to spoil Christmas. Calling someone a Christmas-spoiler was about the worst thing you could say. She wouldn't even say that about them, even though it was true. She didn't care if they walked on and on and didn't come back.

She could go right into the hospital and find a pretty young mother. This mother would play tennis and swim, go to PTA, wear cute clothes and makeup, paint pictures, even have a beauty shop in their house.

She was in there behind those stone walls. So close. The distance was about the same as that from the back door to Pop's shop. It was strange she'd stayed in the hospital so long. If she had tried really hard, she wouldn't be sick. After all, she didn't have tonsillitis or flu or a broken arm.

Still, her mother's sickness must be very serious. No one would tell her. The sunshine-circle ladies and a lot of other people seemed to pity her. The kids at school had shut up, but hadn't forgotten. The least little thing would get them yelling at her again.

Ali realized she didn't know what kind of person was behind those nearby walls. Her own mother was still a stranger to her.

Nana and Pop were coming back. Pop didn't need to wear that old plaid hunting jacket all the time. He had a nice polyester topcoat. And there was Nana—her legs about to freeze in those nylons because she wouldn't wear slacks like other women. At least, she wasn't blubbering anymore. She was stepping right along, full of beans again.

She got into the car. "Ali, we have an idea that will be nice for you. It's just a little way over to Burnt Timbers. We'll take you there, and you can have a visit with Cousin Ted and Cousin Delbert while we're seeing Kathleen. They don't have much company. We'll discuss this insistence of yours with Mr.—the social worker. That's best."

So Nana, not Pop, was the one who had a plan. She'd probably had it all along.

"Now do you think you can be mannerly at Ted and Delbert's?"

Ali didn't answer. She felt like a piece of wet

Kleenex. Her legs ached as if she'd run ten miles. She began to tremble. She tried to do what Mr. Beaumont had once told her to do. She tried to get hold of herself. As Pop swung out onto the highway, she hugged herself against the cold.

11

Burnt Timbers was the tackiest town on earth. One of its streets turned into a muddy road. That's where Ted and Delbert lived in a little blue house. In the past, Ali's visits there had been very brief. Nana had always said she couldn't stand to be in that house more than ten minutes. Now Ali was supposed to stay there all morning and be mannerly, besides.

Ali stood and watched the Chevy pull away. They couldn't even wait to see her into the house. She turned and, with two gift-wrapped fruitcakes under her arm, went up the unshoveled walk. She squeezed by the wringer washer on the front porch and knocked on the door.

Cousin Ted was very surprised to see her and moved big cardboard boxes aside so she could get in the house. Ted and Delbert always seemed to be getting ready to move, but they never did. They kept things: newspapers, magazines, tools, boxes, clothes. They went to lots of auction sales.

"You caught us in kind of a mess." Ted moved a stepladder. "I've been doing some rough carpentry, making cabinets. We don't have a place to put anything. Come out to the kitchen. Delbert went hunting this morning. Near last day of deer season. Got his buck at seven forty-six. He's dressing it out."

Delbert was sharpening a knife on a whetstone. Ted could have made two of Delbert, who was thin and sharp like the big knife in his hand. Ali had always been a little afraid of him.

He looked curiously at her. "What brings you here so early in the morning?"

He got no answer. She wasn't going to give a long-winded explanation of how she wasn't allowed to visit her own mother in Webbs Flats hospital.

"Nana sent you this." She held out the cakes. "I'm supposed to stay here until they come back for me."

"Yes. Well, thanks." Delbert tossed aside a deer shank with the hoof still on. "You take the cakes, Ted. I never told Cousin Betty, but I don't care much for fruitcake."

Ted didn't wait for Christmas. He unwrapped a cake and began to eat.

The bloody meat and its raw game smell made Ali feel sick. Ted's eating an entire fruitcake with nothing to go with it didn't help much either. Ali hugged her arms again. She had to get hold of herself.

They talked of road conditions and of Delbert's luck for the past three deer seasons. Still, time dragged. Ted thought of another subject. "How do you like Burnt Timbers?" he asked Ali.

"I don't like small towns. When I can, I'm going to live out in Montana or somewhere," Ali said.

" 'God made the country, man made the city, and the devil made the small town.' Ever hear that?" Delbert asked. Ali hadn't, and she thought it was neat.

She looked around the kitchen and wondered if there was any way she could escape to the outdoors. She offered to shovel the walk, but Delbert said the snow shovel was lost, under the snow, perhaps.

Twice Ali thought she heard the old Chevy and looked out the window but saw cars pass by. The thought occurred to her that if she didn't live with Pop and Nana, she would have to live in Burnt Timbers and keep house for Ted and Delbert. They were the only other well relatives she knew of.

Ted began to take leftovers out of the refrigerator. Ali told him she didn't want anything to eat. She wished she had asked Nana when they were coming back. It was past lunchtime. She hadn't expected them to be away so long. Something must have happened. Maybe Pop and Nana were killed in a wreck going back to the hospital. The state police were trying to find her, but nobody knew where she was.

Finally there was a lovely sound. No doubt about it, that was the old Chevy stopping out in front. Ali had never thought she could be so glad to see Pop and Nana.

Nana explained to Ted that they couldn't come in for a snack. They had eaten at a place on the highway and had a long drive home with more snow forecast. As Ali got in the car, she handed Nana a stained package. It was wrapped in second-hand holly paper, which Ted had found in a stack back of a door. "Here's a present for you. It's venison steak."

"I declare," Nana exclaimed, smiling. "That's the first present they ever gave me." Ali knew Nana worked hard on presents. She cooked things people didn't like. She made clothes they hated. Ali had never considered that she might expect something in return.

As they left Burnt Timbers, Ali repeated, "'God made the country, man made the city, and the devil made the small town.' Ever hear that?"

"I've heard it," Pop said, "but I don't agree. I think wherever you are you have to make peace with God, get along with man, and dodge the devil."

That was neat, too, Ali decided. Doing all that would sure keep a person busy.

Nana turned on the radio to get the latest weather report. Chipmunks were singing "Christmas, Don't Be Late." She left it on. Apparently singing chipmunks didn't make her nervous. Ali had to speak up to be heard. "What did Mr. Pienkowski say?"

"He'd gone to a conference in Albany, so we didn't have a chance to talk with him." Nana's voice was louder than the singing chipmunks. "Your mother is just fine, Ali. A nurse and some attendants said she is one of the best patients they have."

"What does that mean, Nana, a good patient? Isn't she a person?"

"Of course, but she needs care, and she is well taken care of there."

"She's on some new medicine," Pop shouted over the radio.

"We've heard that before, Thurman. Always something new. I don't know how many they've tried, but what she must have is hospital care." Nana turned to look back at Ali. "I know you understand that." She noticed the undelivered gift on the seat beside Ali. It seemed to remind her of something. "I can't tell you flat out what your Christmas gift will be, Ali, but it's something very special."

Nana would try to make up for not letting her visit her mother. She'd give her a dog, as if something alive would do the trick. "I don't want another dog."

"Oh, it's no dog. Something more expensive, not cheap, I'll tell you."

Whatever the present was, Ali wasn't going to like it.

Nana turned down the radio. "Now don't beg me to tell," she said.

"I didn't say anything, Nana."

"How did you get along with Cousin Ted and Cousin Delbert?"

"Okay."

"I think it's a downright shame that Ted has trouble getting steady work," Nana said.

"Ted ought to be a teacher," Ali announced. "Just by sleeping late one morning, he taught me to read. If it wasn't for Ted, I'd probably be an Astro. That's the slow verbal-arts group."

Nana sighed. "Ali, sometimes you get the strangest notions and say the oddest things."

Pop had turned on the headlights, but there was still enough daylight for Ali to see the lovely pattern of her willow tree against the overcast sky. On River Street the big plastic candles hanging from the lamp posts swayed in the wind. They had just

90

been put up by the Merchants Committee, and for weeks they would be buffeted by every wind that blew. Ali sometimes felt as helpless as those candles: she couldn't direct what happened to her or which way she turned either.

"Stores are open evenings now," Nana remarked.

The sight of Christopher's reminded Ali of the gift she'd bought. She had no use for it anymore. At least she could do something; she could take it back. "Let me out here, Pop. There's something I have to do downtown. Then I'll bomb on home."

Pop stopped at the traffic light, and Ali was out of the car before Nana could protest or ask any questions.

In Christopher's the clerk who had sold Ali the blouse seemed wearier than ever. When Ali returned the blouse in its gift box, she nodded, unsurprised. "So you've decided to get a larger size? We still have this style in large, so it will be no trouble."

"No, I don't want to exchange it. I don't need it now. The person I got it for—well, that person died."

The clerk was startled. "Died! Oh, I'm sorry. Who was it?"

"She doesn't live here."

"Oh. Well, in that case. . . . Now if it was the

wrong size, you could exchange it. But if a person dies, I don't know. I'll have to check with Mr. Christoper. Just a minute."

Ali couldn't break down and bawl in Christopher's sportswear department, but that's what she felt like doing. She wasn't so mad at Nana anymore—although Nana must have used up her 10 percent of unreasonableness for the entire year—but the day had completely disappointed Ali's expectations. Maybe it had been sad for Nana and Pop, too.

She wandered over to the card rack and found herself at the section with cards for mothers. One read: A gift for you, Mother dear. It showed a package inside a mailbox.

Not waiting for the clerk to come back, Ali darted out of the store. By the time she got to the post office, it was four minutes before closing time. Fortunately, there was no line at the postal window. That would come later, nearer Christmas. She felt again in her jacket pocket to make sure the tam purse was there. There just had to be enough money in it.

The blouse was feather light and fit easily into the post-office mailer she bought. At the high desk, using a pen on a chain, she addressed it to Kathleen Doyle, Webbs Flats State Hospital. Under the word *From* in the upper left corner, she squeezed her own name and address. The postal clerk weighed it, gave her a few cents change, and closed the window.

Ali bounded down the post-office steps, paying no attention to icy spots. As she ran under a street light, she jumped so high she almost touched its plastic-candle decoration. She wondered how she could have felt so miserable a few hours ago. That she could change so quickly was something she intended to remember. No telling when she might need to know somthing useful like that.

12

On Christmas morning, Ali's gift was not in the living room beneath the Scotch pine she and Pop had decorated. The kitchen was the only place big enough for a bicycle.

It was a beautiful, white ten speed. Nana emphasized that it was the best, nothing cheap about it. She had picked something very hard to dislike.

Bobbi came over later to show off all the Barbie-doll stuff she had received for Christmas. Besides a lot of new outfits, she had a Barbie beauty shop and a Barbie recreational vehicle.

"I like to play Barbie because I do as I want with this stuff," Bobbi said. "For one thing, nobody better mess up this beauty shop. I've got it the way I want it."

Bobbi came to play every day during vacation.

When Ali got bored playing Barbie doll, she announced she was a customer under a dryer, took one of the books she'd borrowed from St. Stephen library, and read. Bobbi didn't mind. She carried on alone as Barbie and as several customers in need of perms, cuts, rinses, and root jobs.

Vacation gave Ali more time to read, and she checked out stacks of books from the library. Nana said it was a downright shame she couldn't ride her new bike to the library, but there was too much snow. She walked instead, always after three o'clock and always with a dime in her jacket pocket. If she checked out more books than she could carry, she called from the pay phone and asked Pop to drive her home.

From books she learned that she was like many of the heroines. Most of them lacked a father or mother, sometimes both. They were looked after by wolves, lived in hollow trees, boxcars, and old schoolhouses. Very few were like Bobbi Clark, with a regular mother and father, living in a regular ranch house with an attached garage and a camper for vacations.

Most of the book heroines, however, escaped regular school. Unfortunately, Ali didn't and was back at her desk soon enough.

With all the Christmas decorations gone, the

classroom looked drab. So did the outdoors, where sleet and rain fell on piles of dirty snow.

The weather was so bad that Mrs. Clark came by after school to pick up Bobbi in their car. She beckoned to Diane and Ali to get in, too. The front seat was piled high with store bags. "You'll have to get in back," she said. "I've got the front seat full of bargains."

"What did you get me, Mom?" Bobbi asked.

"You'll see. Some real cute things at January sales, half price. Some nice slacks and long-sleeved tops."

"My mother is getting me a lot of stuff, too," Diane said. "What are you getting new, Ali?"

"I don't know."

"They don't make leggings your size." Diane giggled. "Too bad. You need them because Nana makes you wear dresses all the time."

"She does not!" Diane had a nerve bad-mouthing Nana. Ali wanted to clobber her, but she couldn't start a ruckus in Clarks' car.

However, Diane turned out to be some kind of fortune-teller. When Ali got home, Nana was sewing. She hummed a little tune as she put away her Singer portable. "I can truthfully say I accomplished a lot today." Nana tied sewing scraps into a little bundle. "I lengthened five of your school dresses. I let them out full hem allowance and put on contrasting bands of plain color. I know you don't like ruffles. The bands make a nice trim. With new leotards and your sweater, these cotton dresses will get you through this winter."

Ali looked at the stack of much-laundered dresses with bright new wide borders on the bottom. She wasn't going to wear them. No way!

"How are you and Mr. What's His Name getting along?" Nana asked.

"Do you mean Mr. Beaumont? That's not hard to remember."

"Of course. I sometimes have a little trouble now recalling names."

"I know. There's a big family of those What's His Names."

Nana shook her head. "I read an article that said after fifty you lose about half a million brain cells a day."

Ali glanced at the floor, as if expecting to see heaps of cells. "Pop thinks you're still awful smart, Nana. He said you were the smartest one when you were in high school."

"It wasn't a very big class, and that was a long time ago. There have been a lot of changes. Still, we have to eat three times a day, so take your dresses up and then come set the table."

As Ali hung the dresses in her closet, she decided which one was the least faded.

The next morning she wore it when she went to stop for Bobbi on her way to school.

There was a smell of shampoo when Bobbi opened the door. She turned to model her new outfit. "Hunter-green slacks and hunter-and-heather top to coordinate." Bobbi stared at the bright extension on Ali's dress. She pointed to the plastic bag Ali carried. "What's that?"

"You'll see. Can I use your room for a minute?"

Ali came out in her jeans and T-shirt. "I left my dress in your room. I'll change before I go home, and you don't need to tell anybody."

"Did you hang it in my closet? I don't want my room messed up," Bobbi said.

At the end of the day, Nana was impressed with how fresh Ali's dress stayed. "Of course, they are permanent press and don't muss as they once did," she said. "Why, I used to iron all day long when Kathleen was—" Nana broke off.

Ali thought of the old photos in the locked drawer. The girl with long braids seemed always to wear a freshly ironed dress. Maybe Nana would like some of that ironing time back.

13

Nana always put the mail on the little telephone table beside the stairway. She was standing next to it when Ali burst in from school and quickly shut the front door against the snow and cold wind.

Nana pointed to an envelope that lay on the table. "Here's a letter for you. I didn't open it, because that's one thing I don't do—open other people's mail."

Ali dropped her math book, her jacket, and cap on the floor. Nana nudged her over so that the melt from her boots soaked into the worn throw rug instead of the varnished floor.

Ali picked up the letter and read the return address. It was from her mother. "Where's the letter opener? I don't want to tear this envelope." Her voice squeaked with excitement.

Nana opened the table drawer. "It's here, right where it always is." Nana tapped the palm of her hand with the blade of the opener. "I don't know what you've been up to that you'd get this letter. You'd better leave well enough alone, I'll tell you. I know you'll realize that someday when you can understand, when it's all explained to you."

"Gimme the opener." Ali slit the envelope and read:

Dear Daughter,

I have been a long time waiting to thank you for the beautiful gift, which is a perfect fit. I didn't write for a while, because I am out of practice and because it is hard for me to write to someone I love, and yet I do not know.

The gift was like a miracle because it told me you knew of me and that I am like a person to you. I take new medicine now. I have talked to the doctor here about you and to my friends and to Mr. Pienkowski. Lots of my old friends have left this place. Someday I might come back to St. Stephen, and we will go around town and have a good time.

Love, Your Mother

Ali read and reread the letter. She was in a trance of joy when she handed it to Nana.

Nana read it, then took off her glasses to wipe her eyes. "She still writes a good hand. So you sent her a present."

"You wouldn't let me give it to her, so I mailed it. And now she can come here to see me. Leave the hospital, the way her friends have," Ali said happily.

The frown mark creased Nana's forehead. She sank wearily into a living-room chair. "You remember that story you had about Pandora's box? If you start begging for her to come home, building up useless hopes, it will be just like opening that box. No end of disappointments and worry. I know; I've been through it. You don't understand now, Ali."

Nana refolded the letter. "It took a long, long time for her to be able to write a letter like this. Now if you put a lot of stress and strain on her, it will all be undone. You sent her a gift; she wrote and thanked you. Leave it that way. Remember, she cooperates at the hospital. She is a very good patient."

"But she's glad I thought of her as a person. She said my gift was like a miracle," Ali cried.

"We'll see about that." Nana studied the writing on the envelope.

"Give me my letter," Ali demanded. She ran up to her room, which she had begun to think of it as their room, hers and her mother's, a shared room. Now she knew her mother was a kind person who could write a nice, friendly letter, same as anybody else. Just knowing that letter was in its special place in the dressing-table drawer made Ali feel calm and glad, the way she had felt when she had smelled the perfume dregs in the little bottle.

Ali wanted to show the letter to Pop and talk privately with him about it, but he didn't go out to his shop that evening. He sat in the living room and finished reading the *St. Stephen Sentinel*. Even though he seemed to read every last word in the *Sentinel*, and Ali didn't care a pin for much that was in the paper, Nana always read aloud selected items she wanted to emphasize.

"It says right here," she began, "'Citizens of Webbs Flats are alarmed and apprehensive that patients from the state hospital now go freely about the village. "Voluntary patients have certain civil rights which we cannot violate," Dr. So-and-So asserts.'" Nana shook her head. "Now just listen to this. 'A long-time resident of Webbs Flats says he now feels he must lock his doors when he leaves his house, something he had never done until the present. A store manager complains that patients come in, buy things, and he can't tell them from customers. A group of residents concerned about change in practices, which allow patients freedom to come and go at the hospital, have requested a meeting with state representative What's His Name to see what can be done about the situation.'

"I should think so," Nana said. "I declare, I don't know what to make of it. It's not the way it used to be at all."

"That's for sure," Pop agreed.

"They don't know what they are letting get started over there at Webbs Flats."

Nana could say anything that she wanted to. It didn't matter to Ali, who had a letter that her mother had written to her personally.

14

Ali wanted to tell Bobbi about the letter, but decided it was too risky. No telling what Bobbi might blurt out in front of Diane or the other kids. Ali was not going to get into another fight, just when everybody had forgotten the September battle. She didn't think about that awful day often either, and when she did, it wasn't so sickening.

She wondered what her mother would think if she knew Ali had once fought the whole class. Nana had never even talked to her about it. At least, she had done something to defend her mother.

She'd done something to receive her letter, too— something better than hitting. Even if she didn't tell anyone about the letter, she felt happy just thinking of it. She remembered the fake autobiography she had written at the start of the school year. Never again would she say her mother was dead, not after receiving a letter from a real live mother.

When they had a unit on the Friendly Letter in verbal arts, Ali studied the examples carefully. The final assignment was to write one. Mr. Beaumont said that they all probably had letters to answer.

Ali had only one, which Nana had said to leave unanswered. Well, that wasn't very polite. She guessed a mother was a friend.

She wrote the heading in the proper place, then the salutation, Dear Friend. Except for one misspelled word and a couple of commas, Mr. Beaumont couldn't find anything wrong. When he went on to the next desk, Ali erased "Friend" and wrote "Mother."

After school, she hurried to change at Clarks' and raced home to find an envelope and stamp. A February thaw had cleared the streets of snow, so she rode her bike to the post office. She was home again by the time Nana called her to set the table.

Nana put a tea bag in the pot. "You haven't said much about school lately."

"Today we had to write a friendly letter. I wrote to my mother."

Nana put the kettle down on the stove burner with a clatter. "You didn't show it to Mr. What's His Name, did you?"

"Mr. Beaumont? Yes, but I had "dear friend" at

the top. It was supposed to be a friendly letter. Tomorrow we might have to write an unfriendly letter."

"But with a new teacher and all, no need to bring up things."

"We don't need to worry about him, Nana."

"Well, people talk. Anyhow, that letter was just a school exercise."

"It was a real letter. I mailed it," Ali said with satisfaction. "Took ten cents."

"Mailed it! What did you write?"

"I told her what I was going to do this summer, and I asked her to come home whenever she wanted. I said she could have her room, *our* room."

"Well, we'll see about that."

Ali expected an answer to her letter, and she looked for one on the little table each day. Saturdays she watched for the mailman herself, but no letter from her mother came. The first Saturday in March, she took a handful of mail from the box. Among the bills, she glimpsed a long envelope, which seemed to have a state emblem on it.

Nana slid it out of the stack. "I'll take that. It's another one of *those* letters."

"Let me see that," Ali demanded.

"It's addressed to Pop and me."

"It's about *my* mother," Ali yelled.

"Just simmer down, Ali. You take care of your mail; I'll take care of mine."

Ali stomped upstairs. Sometimes Nana was downright impudent.

Each day Nana watched Ali come in from school and look through the scant mail on the table. "I'll tell you something I've learned," she said. "When things don't go the way you want, best get your mind on something else."

That evening Nana read aloud an ad from the *Sentinel*. Spring baton classes were to be given by a gym teacher, who would organize a girls' baton-twirling drill team also. Even though lessons weren't cheap, Nana said Ali could enroll. That was supposed to get her mind on something else.

It did for a few minutes. She thought of herself marching down a street lined three-deep with people. All the other twirlers had beautiful, long, flowing hair, but hers was shorter than a boy's. She imagined she heard a jarring thud. A spectator sneered. "Look at Ali. Just dropped her baton. Jeez, is she tall!"

Ali shook her head to rid herself of that awful picture. She knew one thing for sure. She wasn't going to take baton and make a fool of herself, not even if Nana bugged her.

But Nana didn't insist. She began to concentrate on herself rather than on Ali. She said she sometimes felt weak as a cat. When she came home with groceries, she was all in but the shoestrings. Ali had to bring in bags and help put groceries away. She tried to save Nana steps by answering the phone and the door when she was home.

One afternoon when Ali came in from school, Nana was lying on the sofa, not doing a solitary thing. "Is it snowing again?" she asked.

"Yes, great big flakes." Ali brushed some off her jacket.

"March snow is the worst. Right at the tag end of winter." Nana had taken off her glasses and didn't look natural.

"Do you want me to do anything?"

"Later on you can go down cellar and get a jar of tomatoes for supper. And, of course, set the table."

Ali went upstairs to work on a project. She was redesigning the get-well card Mrs. Clark had sent her long ago when she had tonsillitis. It pictured a sick rabbit. Ali was restoring the rabbit to health with colored magic markers, trying to make a nice Easter card to send her mother.

She heard the phone ring and was halfway down the steps when she realized Nana had gotten up from the sofa to answer.

"I don't see how we can," she heard Nana say. "I'm far from well just now. Yes, it would be somewhat. We don't have extra room. We're not made out of money. . . . I'm not able to contend with it right now. . . . No, I don't think we should try it, not this spring. I can't start it all again." Nana hung up the phone.

Ali grasped the stair spindles. "Was that the hospital? Was it Mr. Pienkowski?" she yelled.

Without answering, Nana went back to the sofa.

"It was! My mother wants to come home for Easter, and you said No." Ali shook the stair spindles hard—shook them and shook them—until the nails that held them cracked loose.

Nana looked up. "No use having a conniption fit."

"You should let her come!" Ali cried.

"You'll have a whole lot easier time in life if you don't try to figure out what other people should do," Nana said wearily.

Ali ran down the stairs, out the front door, and up the slushy sidewalk. She had to do something, and there was nothing she could do but run.

She ran down the hill, beside the park, along Main Street, and turned into a narrow side street. She didn't pay attention to where she was going, but her pace gradually slowed to a trot. Shivering with cold, she came to the end of the sidewalk on the side street that led into Route 86.

Why, there was her willow tree! It stood in front

of her as if the world were just the same. She'd never seen it more beautiful. Each snow-edged twig was a faint yellow-green. The first sign of spring had come. Things stayed the same, and things changed.

It was getting colder. Her feet were soaking wet; she was freezing. She would have to go back.

There was still plenty of daylight. Ali had reached the park when she saw someone coming toward her through the snow. She could tell by the droop of the shoulders it was Pop. He carried her ski jacket and shoe boots. Without a word, she held on to his arm while she changed into the boots. They started up the hill toward home.

"I got awful mad at Nana," Ali finally said.

"So I hear."

"Can't you make her let my mother come home?"

"Nana seems to be under the weather right now."

"What's the matter with her?"

"I don't know. She doesn't complain much, but I can tell."

"I felt as if I had to do something."

"Tell you one thing you can do. You can help me nail the stair rail back in place."

"I'm sorry, Pop. Once you said Nana did okay ninety percent of the time. Well, maybe she does, but when she's wrong, she's one hundred percent wrong."

15

Bobbi was going to take baton and could hardly wait for lessons to start. She spent her entire savings on a Barbie baton-twirler outfit, complete with little baton.

In the afternoons, Ali felt silly trying to walk home with Bobbi, who didn't really walk. She strutted and threw an imaginary baton, waited a long time for it to come down from a great height, then caught it casually. She reminded Ali there was one place left in the class.

"I don't care. I'm not going to take baton. I'll be busy with other stuff," Ali said.

"Like what?"

"Oh, I don't know. Well, for one thing—" Ali thought for a bit, then asserted, "My mother is coming for a visit. She's taking some new medicine. She's a lot better."

"Your mother!"

"She talked to Mr. Pienkowski about it."

"Who's that?"

"The social worker at the hospital."

"What does he do?"

"He doesn't *do* anything. He just *is* somebody."

"He must do something."

"Talks to people, I guess."

"Does he get paid?"

"Sure."

"My mother talks to people, and she *does* something at the same time. She makes people look decent. That's what I'm going to do."

"I know."

As they passed Diane's house, she ran out shouting, "I get to take, Bobbi. Mom put me in baton. I begged and begged, and she called the teacher today, and it was the last place."

"See there, Ali. I told you," Bobbi said.

Diane marched down the sidewalk, stepping high. "It's just too bad, Ali. You should have called in."

"I don't care. I've got other things I'm going to do."

"I'll bet," Diane retorted. "What are you going to do? Raise more freak punkins?"

"Going to do that and something else, too."

"I'll bet."

"I am," Ali insisted.

"What?"

"I'm going to—um—ah—" Ali's puzzled expression changed to a brighter look. "I'm going to have a school. You know how some kids don't learn to read right away? Nana saw an article about it in the *Sentinel*. It will be for those kids that didn't learn to read the first time around."

Diane put her hands on her hips. "Oh, is that so? Well, we'll send you your first victim. My little brother Jonathan!"

"Fine. It'll be the Fat Ted School of Catch-up Reading," Ali announced. "You send Jonathan over."

"It's a dumb name for a school, but we'll send him *anywhere* to catch up with his class."

Ali wanted to get a lot of bike rides in before her Fat Ted School began. She pedaled all around St. Stephen. When she rode beside the park, she had a queer feeling. She was sure her mother had ridden on a new bike on the same street. It was the same feeling she often had when she sat at the dressing table in the shared room. The dressing table was still there, but what had become of her mother's bike? Even Nana wouldn't give a good thing like that to the rummage.

❊   ❊   ❊

113

As usual, Ali was very careful about her bike lock when she rode to school on the last day. There wasn't much to do that final day, but they had to go all the same. After books and equipment were put away, with Bobbi supervising, Mr. Beaumont took the class to the park to play softball.

Ali sat down on the grass beside Mr. Beaumont. "I wish you could be our teacher again next year in sixth grade," she said. "You don't make me think you know more about me than I know about myself."

"Well, I don't, Ali. 'Know thyself,' to quote Billy S. Don't you believe you've made progress in that direction since the day you got your nickname?"

"Sometimes I get an awful backset. You see, my—"

"Oh, Mr. Beaumont," Diane interrupted. "Did you see how I struck out? I don't care. Say, did you know that Bobbi and I are taking baton? Then, in junior high, I'm going out for color guard. So's Bobbi. We're sure to make it, because we're in baton. Ali, maybe you could go out for something else—something you need to be tall for."

Eric Huskey yelled at Diane, and she ran to her place in the outfield.

Ali pulled a grass stem. "I don't want to go out for anything until I finish this . . . this knowing about my mother, maybe even my father, and knowing myself. Then junior high would be different."

"True, Ali," Mr. Beaumont agreed. "I've met your grandparents. Nice folks. I trust you talk it over with them?"

"Not much. Sometimes it's hardest to talk over heavy stuff with the people who are nearest you. It's kind of there, but you don't talk about it, because if you do, you might yell and break things loose. If I ask Nana anything, she says I'll understand later on, or she gets sad or mad. Pop doesn't want to make her upset, maybe not get his supper or anything. She's been sick, besides. So sometimes I think things up."

Ali hoped the kids wouldn't notice she was not playing ball. There was something else she wanted to tell Mr. Beaumont. "My room was my mother's room, too. Sometimes, when I sit at the dressing table, she seems to be right in the room with me. Do you think that's spooky?"

"No, not if you know she's really not there."

"She's at Webbs Flats, Mr. Beaumont."

"That's not out of this world."

"I know. I was over there once. It's not so far. When I think about that, she seems real. She wrote me a friendly letter." Ali looked down at the grass.

"Then I get this other notion that she's far away, that I can never reach her. I just imagine different kinds of mothers for myself. Is that scary?"

"Doesn't scare me, Ali. Sometimes we do that with people we know very well. We imagine them worse than they are, or we try to make them perfect so they'll deserve our love. But finally we see them as they are and usually accept them—their good ways, bad ways, warts and all. Like those pumpkins you grew."

Ali smiled. "I'm putting in a big crop of them this summer."

Bobbi had finished policing the area and noticed that Ali had Mr. Beaumont's attention. "Ali Doyle," she shouted, "get up to bat. Or are you too stuck-up to play ball?"

Ali went to the plate, swung, and got the first good hit of her entire life.

16

Ali was upstairs, selecting supplies for her school, when Nana answered the door. "Diane's little brother is here," she called up to Ali. "He wants you. Won't say why."

Ali gathered up the scrap paper, magic markers, and picture books she had prepared and raced down.

Jonathan had raveled-rope blond hair like his sister. For a little kid, he looked awful glum. "I don't want to go to school in summer," he said.

"It's not like regular school," Ali said. "Come on, we'll go outside in the backyard."

Ali sat down on a part of the lawn shaded by the shop. Jonathan glared down at her. "I'll do numbers, but I won't read," he said.

"What if you want to read about numbers?" She patted the ground. "Have a seat. Now, for a start, say this with your mouth open: fat Ted is not up."

Jonathan clamped his lips shut. He looked as if he might not open his mouth until lunchtime. Finally, he muttered, "Why?"

"Open up. Say it. Then I'll tell you. It's something Diane doesn't know."

He uttered those lovely sounds. Ali explained their importance. She kept right on those vowels until Jonathan began to fidget. He pointed to the shop. "What's in there?"

"It's Pop's shop. I'll let you look in, but don't monkey with anything. See how this door latch works?"

Jonathan surveyed the orderly shop. "This place is really neat."

"Don't touch anything!" Ali picked up a booklet that was fastened to the workbench with string. "See this? Instruction for operation of Model 79-G? You'd have to be able to read all of this before you could work in a shop."

Jonathan opened his mouth. "A, e, i, o, u."

"Shut your mouth, Jonathan, before you swallow a fly. That's all for today. See you tomorrow."

She wasn't sure he'd show up, but he did. He came the next day and each morning for the rest of the week. He even forgot and came on Saturday. No doubt about it, Jonathan was catching up.

At the end of the second week, Ali had another

treat for him besides inspections of Pop's shop. "Now that you can read, Jonathan, we're going to the library and get you some good books."

"I don't want books about elves. I want to read about motorcycles. Do they have any about motorcycles and snowmobiles?"

"Sure. Come on."

The reputation of Ali's catch-up school spread. The third week Jonathan showed up with two friends who enrolled. For Ali, it was like playing school, only better. She was always teacher.

After the morning session of the Fat Ted Catch-up School, Ali was free to ride off on her bike. Bike rides weren't always just for fun, either. Nana didn't feel like traipsing all over town, going to the bank and paying gas, electricity, and water bills. So Ali did these errands on her bike, which was a lot more interesting than setting the table.

At first the high ceiling and thick carpet of the bank intimidated her. She was afraid she'd make a mistake. At least, she was tall enough to be noticed in front of the teller's high window.

"Good afternoon, Ali." She jumped at the deep voice. Ali turned and saw Bryan Jones's father look back and smile at her as he crossed the lobby to his big desk. She relaxed. If the bank was a place where people like Mr. Jones worked, no need to be so up-tight.

On her way home from town, Ali usually stopped at the library to fill her bike basket with books for herself, for Nana, and for the Catch-up School.

Nana had taken to reading things besides the *Sentinel* lately. It had been a long time since she'd read novels, but she said she was too lazy and ornery now to do much else. Ali selected books for her very carefully. Nana stayed loyal to authors she'd liked when she last took time to read—about thirty years ago, Ali estimated. Once Ali brought her a very new novel. Nana was shocked and said she didn't know what the world was coming to. Ali brought no more of those books.

Though the summer days were longer, they seemed to go faster than winter days. It would soon be time for school. Ali was glad she hadn't depended on Bobbi for amusement during the summer. Baton was almost a full-time job for her; she had to practice, twirl, drill, compete.

One morning, however, Ali was surprised to answer the doorbell and find Bobbi twirling her baton. "I haven't got much time, Ali," she said breathlessly. "Has your mother come yet?"

"Not yet." Ali dodged the twirling baton.

"You better find out when she's coming, so you can make plans."

"I've got plans."

"It better be pretty soon if it's going to be this

summer. Christopher's has those back-to-school signs up already."

"I know. They can't wait."

Bobbi took a long breath. "You know, I'm not allowed to tell anything I hear in my mom's beauty shop, but I didn't hear this there. This lady was talking to Mom out on the porch when she was leaving. You know how they think my mom knows about everybody in St. Stephen? This lady was trying to locate the people in her high-school class for a reunion. It was your mother's class because they said, 'No, guess she couldn't come.' Then this lady said, 'How about Mark Doyle?' Then my mom said, 'You can cross him off your list. Nobody knows where he is.' That's what my mom said." Bobbi looked at Ali expectantly.

Ali was indignant. "That's a big help! You've twirled until you're dizzy. First place, it's not one bit true. I've looked at my mother's class pictures five thousand two hundred and eighty times. There's no Mark Doyle in that class."

Bobbi was insulted. "Oh, well, if you already know so much." She turned sharply and went off down the street, twirling her baton.

17

Near the end of summer, the Merchants Committee always held St. Stephen Harvest Days, when stores put bargains on the sidewalk and people had booths for selling.

Ali filled out the application blank that Nana showed her in the *Sentinel*, and soon she was assigned a booth to sell warty pumpkins right in front of Christopher's. Jonathan wanted to help. He'd been watching the pumpkins grow all summer.

When Harvest Days arrived, Pop and Jonathan helped Ali set up the booth early in the morning. She didn't have to stay in it every minute, for Jonathan was reliable and good at making change.

Ali strolled among the other booths, and then came back to give Jonathan his turn. She hadn't been there long when she heard a familiar voice.

"Ah, at last. Something unique and appealing. I'll have this grotesque number." It was Mr. Beaumont.

"I didn't see you all summer!" Ali exclaimed.

"Among other things, I returned to my native heath. How was summer, that queen of seasons, for you?"

"It was a super summer." Ali thought for a moment. "I don't know why exactly. We didn't go anywhere. When Pop got vacation, he stayed home and insulated our attic. And the special thing I thought might happen. . . . Well, it didn't."

Ali stopped to wait on a customer. Then she turned back to Mr. Beaumont. "I guess this summer seemed good because some things worked, like the reading school I had. I made it work. Jonathan and the other kids learned a lot. They can keep up now. Diane's mother sent me five dollars with a card that said it was well worth it. Some of the other mothers did, too. That's what I'm using for my school clothes, that and my share of this booth. I have to split with Jonathan. Then, too, this summer I did a lot of work for my grandmother."

"Work!" Mr. Beaumont pretended amazement.

"I did things myself." Ali realized she felt proud. "I began to feel that I can make things happen instead of just seeing what is going to happen to me."

Mr. Beaumont nodded. "It's a good feeling. I can see that you have indeed had a super summer."

Mr. Beaumont went down the street with a warty pumpkin under each arm. He was a walking ad for their booth, and soon a number of cash customers came along and bought them out.

"Jonathan, let's count the money," Ali said. "I think our profits are going to be just short of enormous."

Jonathan opened their cashbox. "Okay, I'll figure my part, forty cents of each dollar."

"That's your percent," Ali agreed.

As soon as they divided the money, Ali headed for Christopher's to spend her share. She bought a pair of slacks, two T-shirts, new jeans, fabric, and a pattern.

At home, Nana examined the garments carefully, turning them inside out to look at the seams. She made no comment, but resumed reading the *Sentinel*.

Ali felt like snatching the paper right out of her hands, but she reminded herself that Nana didn't feel well. Anyway, why should she care whether Nana liked her clothes or not? She liked them. Ali wanted to see the *Sentinel* herself. Any day the list of grades and teachers would be published. She wanted to know who her teacher would be.

Nana continued to study the paper closely. She

read aloud about a lady who set fire to her house with a pot roast. Slowly she turned a page. "It says right here," she remarked, " 'Board of Education eliminates special services.' " Nana read on. " 'Due to budgetary cuts, St. Stephen school system will not have a number of pupil-service programs this year. The Board of Education finally approved the recommendation of What's His Name, chairman of the finance committee, at a special meeting last night. The position of elementary guidance counselor was abolished in an economy move. Lisa Rosengren, who held this position, has accepted a regular classroom assignment in the school system.' "

"Turn to the next page, Nana. See who's teacher of Grade Six, South Range."

They both saw the name at the same time. "I guess you get the counselor, Ali, Lisa Rosengren. I know a lot of Rosengrens, but don't recall any Lisa. Is she Miss or Mrs.?"

"Who knows? But she's flexible and a good thing, too, because she's going to have kids instead of files this year. *Flexible* is a word she uses a lot."

That word made Ali think of Pop's carpenter saw, which bent and bound if she held it wrong and tried to force it to cut. She'd learned to let it glide. Maybe she could glide right along with Ms. Nodding Noodle.

The thought of the new school year reminded

her of the *Excelsiors*, and she went up to the room to study them again.

Faces—serious, smiling, pretty, plain—regarded Ali as she leafed through the books. In the *Excelsior* of her mother's senior year, a face jumped out from the parade of freshman photographs. There was something about the forward thrust of the head, the skinned-teeth smile, the expression of starting to enunciate that set the girl apart. It was her all right—Ms. Rosengren, when she was Lisa Larson. She could have known Kathleen McNair. As a freshman, perhaps she had looked up to her mother, who was a senior.

Once again Ali was relieved that she hadn't handed in that pack of lies about being born in Iraq. That was a whole year ago. She wouldn't write anything like that now. Sixth grade was going to be different from fifth.

For one thing, she was not going to change clothes at Clarks'. She'd just wear a new outfit and ask Nana how she liked it before she walked out the door. Besides, she'd bought some material thin enough to spit through and a pattern with many dit-dats. When Nana was feeling better, she could make Ali a frilly dress to wear one hour on Sundays.

Ali's plan worked fine on the first day of school.

Nana didn't say anything about her new outfit. Diane had something new, too—a big plastic purse that she swung around herself as she walked home with Bobbi and Ali.

"What's that purse for?" Ali asked.

"For anything I want, like this." Diane took out a tightly folded square of paper. "I'll have a lot of these before the year is over, and I'll need some place to keep them. This is from Eric Huskey. He passed it to me in music. He says he likes me."

"Don't answer it!" Bobbi shrieked.

"Why not?"

"He'd carry your note around in his pockets. They're so full, it would fall out, and Ms. Rosengren would read it out loud to the whole class. I think she's just the kind that would."

"So what?" Diane put the note back in her purse. "I'll bet you haven't got a note from a boy yet this year. Ali won't get any, not when she's taller than every boy in the class . . . besides the other reason."

"What other reason?" Ali demanded, stopping directly in front of Diane's house.

"Whatever reason they might have," Diane said, and turned in to her walk.

Ali took a tightly folded square of paper from the pocket of her loose-leaf notebook. "I didn't want to tell Diane, but I got a note from Chad, that new boy."

"What does it say?"

"It says he goes with his big brother to a dump to shoot rats and that I can go with them whenever I want."

18

It was handy for Ali to be able to wear what she wanted to school, but it sure was odd. Nana didn't seem to care what Ali wore. She wasn't interested in getting out her Singer to lengthen old things or to make new ones. Nana didn't seem to care about a lot of things: rummage was piling up; meals were likely to be fast food; they had not had a pie for a long time.

At breakfast one morning Nana announced, "After all that doctoring, I've finally given in. At ten o'clock this morning, I have to go to St. Stephen General for some tests."

People were always having tests. Ali thought little about it. In the days that followed, she forgot about Nana's appointment.

Then, about a week later, Ali spied a new robe spread out on Nana's bed and new bedroom slippers next to it. She ran downstairs. "Nana, that robe on your bed, did you go out and buy it?"

"Sure did."

"Didn't you feel like making yourself one out of something else?"

"No, and I didn't have time. I need something decent looking now. By four tomorrow afternoon I have to be in the hospital."

"Hospital!" Ali remembered the tests. "What did they show, Nana, those tests?"

"That I should have an operation."

The very word scared Ali. "But, Nana, you don't believe in operations—like you don't believe in allergies and IQ!"

"I know. I always thought I could avoid this operation, thought it was kind of a fad. But when they sit you down there and give you such a talking-to. I declare, if it's not one thing, it's another. Thank goodness, Thurman's family hospitalization at the plant will cover this operation."

"What kind of operation, Nana?"

"Hysterectomy."

"What's that?"

"An operation, that's all, Ali. Set the table."

Hysterectomy sounded like history, but that couldn't be. Ali looked the word up in the Little Web at home. "Hysterectomy, surgical removal of the uterus." Just five words, so maybe it wasn't a very important operation.

At school the next day she looked up the word in Big Web, but got no more information. She knew about the uterus from a movie they had in health. She concentrated on the five words of the definition, counting them on her fingers and repeating them to herself.

Then other questions struck her. Why should it be removed? What had those tests shown? She knew about cancer from health, too. It must be that Nana had cancer. Ali had to get home before Nana left for the hospital. She'd make Nana tell her. As Ali ran ahead of Bobbi and Diane up the hill, she felt as if she couldn't breathe or swallow.

The house was empty, and there was no note. Ali ran upstairs. Things had been cleared off Nana's dresser; the new robe wasn't in her closet. Nana had packed her suitcase and gone.

The house was too desolate and lonesome, so Ali stayed outside. She was clearing away frosted pumpkin vines when Pop drove up. She ran to the car. "Pop, she's already gone."

"Yes, she called me at work. Said she was kind of nervous and wanted to get over there. A church-circle friend drove her. I'll change clothes and go to make sure she's settled in all right."

Ali followed him into the kitchen. "I know what the operation is, but why does Nana need it?"

"Doctor's orders, you might say."

"Pop, I really want to know."

"I do, too, Ali." Pop looked very serious. "But nobody knows for sure until after the operation tomorrow."

"Shouldn't we tell my mother about Nana?"

"We'll tell her after it's over, when Nana's well again." Pop was trying hard to be cheerful. "I'll be home about suppertime."

Ali knew a good supper might make Pop feel better. "What shall I fix for your supper, Pop?"

They looked in the refrigerator. "I guess Nana didn't feel like getting in groceries," Pop said. He opened the freezer compartment. "Nothing here but soup meat. Hot vegetable soup would be good."

"It's frozen hard as a rock, and it takes a long time to cook soup meat and then put in vegetables," Ali said.

"We could use the pressure cooker. You know that's what Nana does when she forgets to thaw. Will you be all right if I go now?"

Ali nodded, but she wasn't so sure. She knew Pop was worried. So was she. The house didn't seem right at all. Nana would be away no telling how many days and nights.

Ali took out the pressure cooker. She didn't know

much about using it. Nana always made her keep her distance as the petcock on the lid jiggled with the pressure of steam. As a reading teacher, however, she could find the book of instructions, read and follow them.

She put the soupbone in the cooker and poured in the required amount of water. After double-checking the instruction booklet, she fitted on the lid, making sure she had the little petcock handy. Sure enough, steam hissed out of the little pipe in the center of the lid. She covered the spitting pipe with the petcock.

Then the telephone rang. Someone asked about Nana. Ali thought it was a lady from Nana's church circle. She seemed to be kind of deaf. Ali talked loud and tried to make her understand that Nana had just gone into the hospital.

She could hear the petcock begin to jiggle. The lady on the phone had been operated on back in 1966. It took a long time to describe the operation and her suffering. The petcock jiggled louder. Ali knew she had to get off the phone and turn down the flame to reduce the steam pressure.

"Have to go now. Bye." She ran to the kitchen. As she reached out to turn down the gas flame, the petcock blew off the pressure cooker. A cloud of hissing steam, greasy water, and meat scraps rose to the ceiling. The lid of the pressure cooker clattered to the stove top. The soupbone flew out, hit Ali in the stomach, and knocked her down. She lay on the floor with the hot bone burning through her shirt.

On shaking legs, she got up and looked at the clock to see how much time she had to clean up. The mess was all over the floor, stove, counter top, and even gommed up on the ceiling.

Coming home to a first-class mess wouldn't help Pop. First Ali tackled it with a rag. She blotted up all the water she could and rinsed the rag in the scrub pail. Nana always said you couldn't beat steel-wool soap pads. Ali grabbed some from the shelf of cleaning supplies. Then she took down the jar of soft oil soap. Why oil cleaned up grease, she didn't know, but those suds worked. She couldn't do anything about the ceiling except hope Pop wouldn't look up there.

The floor, stove, and counter top were clean by the time she met Pop at the door. "You better go to the Colonel's and pick up some chicken. The soup didn't turn out very well."

While he was gone, Ali hurried to wash the burners so nothing would stink when she heated the tea water. Then she put some ice cubes on the big blister on her stomach. She'd have to take care of herself. Pop had enough to worry about.

❊　　❊　　❊

The next morning Ali looked at the *Sentinel* and found Elizabeth McNair listed under hospital admissions. Obituaries were on that page, too, and two of the people who died were the very same age as Nana.

She tried to eat the oatmeal Pop had cooked. "I can't go to school today. Let me stay at the hospital with you, so I'll know when it's over."

"Your job is to go to school. It won't be easy, but do the very best you can."

Ali's best was just being there. She was too troubled to work or listen to Ms. Rosengren.

Once again the house was quiet and empty when she came in from school. Ali recalled with awful regret all those times she'd come home and started a fuss. Get your mind on something else. Keep busy. That's what Nana would say. Ali couldn't think of anything to do in the yard, so she dragged out the vacuum. The place could do with a cleaning. She jumped when the sweeper sent something rolling out from under the dining-room table. It wasn't a fat mouse. It was one of Nana's little bundles of sewing scraps.

Ali thought of all the things Nana had sewed, all the fruitcakes she'd baked. Nana meant to please people with those things. Maybe she'd rather have been doing something else, but she just kept working away, all the time losing brain cells and getting as old as those people in the obituaries. Worst of all, Nana's girl, that she'd ironed all those dresses for, got sick and had to go away. That must have been terrible.

Chad, the new boy at school, had told her his grandparents lived in a condominium in Florida where children couldn't stay more than twenty-four hours. Suddenly something occurred to Ali, something she'd never thought of before. Pop and Nana might want to do something besides take care of her. She tried to think of herself without them, but couldn't.

Now Nana was in the hospital with a factory-made robe, having an operation she had tried not to believe in. Ali began to cry, harder and harder. She didn't care if they heard her clear down at Clarks'.

Ali wasn't aware of the Chevy driving into the garage, and Pop was in the kitchen before she knew it. "It's all right, Ali. Nana came through real well, everything considered. I expected to be home before now with news for you. But it took quite a while, and she was groggy when they brought her back to her room. That's to be expected. You wouldn't believe what she was saying—mumbling about being sorry she didn't have time to make us some frozen casseroles. Now isn't that just like her?"

Ali hugged Pop and laughed through her tears. "It sure is. And she didn't have anything real bad, spread all over, did she?"

"Well, she had a big operation. That's bad enough."

"I mean, what did the doctor tell you? Why did she need that operation?"

"It'll be a while before they get all those lab reports on account of the weekend and all. Friday is not the best day for surgery, I guess. Don't fret now. The operation is over."

Pop hadn't answered Ali's question. She still couldn't take a real deep breath clear to the bottom of her lungs. The air just wouldn't go down. She couldn't eat any of the lasagna Mrs. Clark had sent over, either. Pop said it was good, but she saw he left most of it on his plate.

When the phone rang Saturday morning, Ali jumped to answer it in case it was St. Stephen General. But it was Bobbi. "My mother says you can come and stay all day," she said.

"For a while in the afternoon," Ali answered, "but this morning Pop is going to take me to get groceries."

When Pop came home from the hospital that afternoon, he reported that Nana was doing well.

"She's perked up, Ali. Wants you to bring her some library books. You can go with me to see her Sunday."

On Sunday morning Pop came downstairs wearing his suit, a white shirt, and tie. Ali looked at him fearfully. Pop was going to church. He didn't go to church; Nana went to church. Ali knew he was going because he was worried about Nana.

Pop sprinkled oatmeal on the boiling water. "Don't look so shocked, Ali. I thought we'd go to services today since Nana can't go. We'll see her friends, tell them she's doing fine. Save a lot of phoning."

"That's not all. You're going to pray," Ali accused.

Pop handed her a steaming bowl. "God has His ways. I leave that up to Him. I want to show some faith and to pray for us to be stronger. I don't think the Good Lord or Nana either wants us to be so down-in-the-mouth."

"You mean, we can't flop over like a couple of unstaked tomato plants—or like a couple of frosted pumpkin vines?"

Pop nodded and smiled a little.

"Can we start early," Ali asked, "so there will be time to go out on 86? There's this willow tree there. I want to see it now before all the gold-colored leaves are gone."

19

To look at Nana you couldn't tell that she had ever been operated on. When Pop and Ali went into her hospital room, she was sitting up in her new robe, watching TV. There was no trace of her frown line. She was smiling.

"Thurman, you and Ali just missed the doctor. He got those reports sooner than he expected. I'm fine. He said I had something or other, which means the cells were changing. But if they find that out early, the way they did for me, there won't be any more to worry about. I won't even have to come back here for treatments. He says I'll be feeling a lot better, and I believe him. Now let me give you a hug, Ali. You won't break any stitches."

Ali took a deep breath. It sure felt good to have the air hit bottom.

Nana also said they didn't baby her one bit in

139

the hospital. Already they were making her get up and walk. She'd be home in a few days.

Pop went to see her after work every afternoon. Ali was still alone after school, but the house felt like home again as she got suppers ready for herself and Pop.

All the newspapers were picked up, all the mail was sorted, with Nana's get-well cards on top, all the dishes were washed on the day Nana came home. She was so glad to be there that she went all over the house, looking at everything. The least little thing, like buds on her Christmas cactus, made her happy.

Nana had been home a few days when deer season opened. Pop's whole plant was let out the first day. Ali watched Pop, who always went hunting, clean his rifle. She knew that no woman as old as Nana and so soon out of the hospital could do whatever had to be done with a shot deer. She, Ali, would have to cut it up, cook it, freeze it. She remembered Ted and Delbert's kitchen from the year before and shuddered.

From all the sermons she'd heard, Ali knew it didn't do any good to pray for selfish, mean things; she prayed, anyhow, that Pop wouldn't get a deer.

As her prayer couldn't have been answered, it must have been ignored. Pop came home early and put his gun away. "Didn't even get a shot," he complained. "Got tired tramping. Too many bullets whizzing around, anyhow. No luck, Ali. I guess it's beef stew for supper then. Get out the pressure cooker."

Ali stayed right by the sputtering pot. When Nana got up from her late-afternoon rest, the stew was ready. "My, that smells good," she said, sitting down in the kitchen. "All this waiting on, I'll be getting spoiled. Pop tells me you did very well, Ali, getting in groceries, keeping dishes washed up, handling the pressure cooker and washing machine. Even helped him keep up his hopes. And you had school, besides. We've got extra expense, but somehow we'll manage to get you something very nice for Christmas again this year."

"The extra I want won't cost anything, Nana. Just to see my mother."

"Well, we'll see about that." Nana picked up the *Sentinel*. "I can't understand what's happening. It says right here, 'Hospital population reduced to eight hundred and fifty. Webbs Flats State Hospital currently has eight hundred and fifty patients, a remarkable decrease from the population of some three thousand a few years ago.'" Nana folded the paper and put it aside. "Think of that now. I don't believe they know what they're doing. We accept what has to be; then they change things."

"Who's they?" Ali asked.

"Bureaucrats, that's who. They don't know what it's like, I'll tell you."

"Things do change, Nana. The way you were telling me how they changed here in St. Stephen since your Grandfather Highfield used to have a cow in his yard. And people change in how they think about things. I know I did while you were in the hospital."

20

Ali didn't expect to see Nana out in the cold when she came home from school, but there she was, wrapped up in Pop's old hunting jacket, digging away in her flower bed.

"Wait, Nana," Ali called, "I'll help you."

Nana straightened up. "Thanks, hon, but I have to get my strength back." She looked up at the blue sky. "Such a pretty day for this time of year. It's a good chance for me to set out this mum plant before the ground freezes. My church circle sent it to me when I was in the hospital." She picked withered blooms off the plant. "No use to waste anything."

"You've got other plants, too. Wait and I'll help you with them tomorrow. It's Saturday."

"We're doing something else tomorrow. When

you get dressed in the morning, wear your nice plaid pleated skirt and maroon sweater."

"Why?"

"We're going to Webbs Flats to visit Kathleen."

Ali flung her arms around Nana. "Can I go in this time? Will I really see her?"

"Careful, careful of my glasses. Well, yes. I was lying there in the hospital with nothing to do, and I got to thinking about how you're getting older. Time goes so fast. So, with everybody deviling the daylights out of me, I've given in." Nana put on a dejected air and in a mournful tone imitated Ali's request. "All I want for Christmas. . . . Besides, I did a little shopping today, all I had strength for. They had a good buy on shoes at Christopher's Pre-holiday Fantastic Sale. I got a pair for Kathleen and some other things. I want to take them over."

"Just like that, I'm to go! I can't believe it!"

"Mr. What's His Name over there, the social worker, he needles me all the time, and then Pop with his 'won't do any harm.' It was just too much. So I thought all right, only for a short visit." With her shovel Nana tapped down the soil around the plant. "It will be hard, harder than you realize, Ali."

❀   ❀   ❀

144

Saturday morning was filled with happy, nervous excitement. Ali zipped her pleated skirt up the back instead of up the side. The maroon sweater itched, but had Nana decreed a nylon blouse with ruffles, Ali would not have protested. Nothing mattered, as long as she could see her mother.

On Route 86, Ali glimpsed a trace of her willow tree in the mist. Thick white fog rose from the river valley, but by the time they reached Webbs Flats the sky was clear and blue.

A few red woodbine leaves still clung to the vines on the gray stone walls of the towered hospital building. Brown leaves filled the corners of the entry steps.

Ali's legs felt shaky as she, Nana, and Pop followed an attendant down a dark hallway, which smelled of coffee, medicine, and stale air. He led them to a large, bright room where people sat on blue and yellow plastic chairs and sofas. Everyone stopped talking and looked at the door when Ali, Pop, and Nana came in.

A young woman wearing a light-blue turtleneck blouse and a navy-blue skirt came toward them. She wasn't much taller than Ali. She was pretty, though she looked like Pop, who wasn't really pretty.

Ali felt a kind of panic. She wanted to turn and

145

run outside where the sun shone. A trembling, cold hand grasped hers. Then her mother flung her arms around her. Both Kathleen and Ali gave way to a flood of tears.

"Now, now, this was to be happy," Nana said.

Ali's mother kissed Nana and Pop. "You didn't tell me how grown-up she is, how pretty!"

"Pretty is as pretty does," Nana pronounced.

"She does pretty well, too. Now you take when Betty had that operation. Ali really took hold." Pop looked proudly at Ali.

"I was glad Pop didn't get a deer," she said.

They all laughed as if the remark were extra-funny.

A heavy woman rose slowly from a chair and smoothed her knit dress down over her big hips. She came and stood beside them, staring at Ali. "I think she favors you some, but not so much as you favor your old man, Kathleen."

"I told you they'd bring her. This is Bonnie. She remembers you from other visits."

"You come to take Kathleen home?" Bonnie asked.

"Not today," Nana said.

"Lots been going home or to live outside. I could go if I had a place to go to. I favored my dad. Everybody said so. But he's dead now, and there's nobody. So they say here. . . ." Bonnie began to sob. An attendant led her away.

Kathleen shook her head. "You can never tell about Bonnie. She's been here longer than I have. It's as if she got on a detour. I don't know if she'll ever get back on the main road."

Ali studied her mother's face. There were little fine lines around her eyes and mouth, which weren't in the *Excelsior* pictures. The wispy bangs were gone, but the grave eyes were the same.

They all sat on one of the blue sofas and talked about everything they could think of. Kathleen held fast to Ali's hand. "What are these callouses from?"

"Gripping the handlebars of my ten-speed. Did you have a bike?"

Kathleen thought for a moment. "Yes. Well, sure I did. It was green, wasn't it? Not any speeds, though. We didn't have them in St. Stephen then. Just pedal and hope."

"It was a good bike. Not cheap," Nana emphasized. "And today we brought you a pair of nice dress pumps, Kathleen. Be good for you to wear when the Sunshine Circle comes and gives a party here. But I'm surprised to see you've got a new pair on. Where did you get those heavy, clunky things?"

147

Kathleen held out her feet for inspection. "Bought them myself. Didn't they tell you about my job?"

"You mean your therapy work in the laundry?" Nana asked.

"No, I don't do that anymore. One doctor said it wasn't therapy, after all. He said eight years in the laundry was eight years in the laundry. Soon after I started taking the new medicine, the doctor said I could be cashier in the commissary and get paid for my work. I was afraid to try. I hadn't handled money for a long time. The first day I worked two hours, next day, four. Afterward it was my job."

"A job!" Nana was amazed.

"Last payday Bonnie and I went out to Webbs Flats Discount, and I bought myself these shoes. I like the thick soles. They keep me off damp ground. I go out more now."

"Well, I never! You went out shopping alone!" Nana exclaimed.

"No, Bonnie was with me. It really seemed good to be able to pick out something for myself. I hadn't walked into a store and done that for years. Only trouble I had was with Bonnie. She wanted to buy everything in the store."

Nana handed her the shoe box. "Take these, too. Your shoes aren't a bit dressy."

Kathleen opened the box and looked at the shoes. "No, thanks, Mother. I like mine better. I see you got these at Christopher's, so you can probably take them back."

Nana smoothed the tissue paper around the shoes and replaced the box lid. "I think it's time we left. We don't want to tire you out," she said stiffly.

"I don't get tired over nothing the way I used to."

As they walked toward the door, Nana stood back and scrutinized her daughter. She bent down and gave Kathleen's hem a jerk. "That skirt hikes up in back."

Kathleen threw back her head and laughed. It was one of the loveliest sounds Ali had ever heard. "Mother, you know my skirts never hung to suit you."

"I hate an uneven hem," Nana stated.

"Uneven hems aren't important, not like some other things." Kathleen's voice was tense. "Things like my getting so I can think about living someplace besides this hospital." She grasped Pop's arm. "Take me home with you today. Please, take me today."

An attendant appeared from somewhere. "Why, Kathleen, three visitors today. Aren't you lucky? And when will all of you come again?"

"Before the roads get bad," Pop promised, patting Kathleen's hand.

"Tell me ahead and I'll be packed and ready to

go home with you," Kathleen said in a calmer tone. "I want to wander around St. Stephen again. I'd be no trouble. My medicine has made more difference than you know."

"We'll see about that," Nana said, and led the way down the long hallway.

Ali read the names on the doors as she passed. S. V. Pienkowski, Social Service Department. A head suddenly popped out of that very door. "Oh, Mr. and Mrs. McNair. And this must be Kathleen's daughter." The man looked at Ali with interest. "I saw you signed in. Kathleen's doctor has a few minutes. I'd like you to see him."

"Could it wait till the next visit?" Nana asked. "I don't suppose he has anything new to tell us, and as you can see we have Ali with us. I've had this surgery and I'm about to give out."

"We'll see the doctor today," Pop interrupted. "You can wait in the car, Ali. We won't be long."

As she left the gray stone building, Ali looked up at the windows. Her mother stood at one, waving; then she was gone. Now Ali knew what kind of mother was in that building. She felt as bright as the sunshine on the woodbine leaves. It was like Christmas, the last day of school, and the day she taught Jonathan to read all put together.

When Pop and Nana came out to the car, Ali noticed that Nana was tight-lipped and her frown line was deep. Ali didn't ask the reason, for she didn't want anything to spoil her happiness. She wanted to remember the sound of her mother's laughter. Pop concentrated on driving. Nana said nothing. They went miles before she spoke. "The way that little sawed-off doctor talked to me!"

Pop reached over and patted her arm. "He did light into you kind of hard, Betty."

"Now they've got this new idea of bringing in the whole family. That's what he called it, family therapy. Only he picked on *me*. You got off easy, as usual, Thurman. You'd think *I* was the one couldn't cope from the way he talked," Nana fumed.

"Kathleen looked so well. Seemed fine," Pop said.

"I thought she looked kind of peaked. But seeing her wasn't as bad as I feared, except for that begging to come home just when we left. Ali, don't breath down my neck. Sit back. I'll turn around so you can hear me better." Nana twisted in her seat.

"She always begs to come home, Ali. I've just learned to steel myself against it, because I know it's best she stay. She's a good patient, and she must have constant care. You must realize that. I know it from all we've been through. Of course, they try different kinds of medicine—have to do something—but I know the risks. It'll never be different."

151

"Sounds to me like they have the right treatment finally, Betty," Pop said.

"We'll see about that." When Pop chuckled, she asked, "Now what's there to laugh about?"

"She was right spunky about those shoes. I remember when she couldn't make up her mind about anything."

"I don't know what to make of it." Nana sounded crushed.

21

Monday, on the way to school, Ali told Bobbi and Diane about her visit. "You know, my mother didn't get to come see me last summer, so I went to see her. It was just for a little while, but it made everything different. I won't have to study those old *Excelsiors* anymore, because I know her now. If I were going to pick out a mother, she's just what I would pick."

"You make so much out of it." Diane snorted. "Everybody born has a mother."

"Everybody born has a birthday, too, but it's still special," Bobbi said.

"Ali, you are just stuck-up. After all, your mother is, you know. . . ." Diane dodged and cried, "Ali! Don't you dare."

"Scaredy, I'm not going to hit you. I don't go

around beating on people anymore, even when they say stupid things." Ali went on with her description. "My mother is not much taller than I am. Her hair is. . . ."

Diane interrupted. "But you're leaving out the most important part."

"You don't know anything about it, Diane," Ali said.

"I know she's still in the hospital."

For a brief moment, Ali did feel like smacking Diane. Instead, she got hold of herself, and they went on to school.

All day, however, Ali couldn't concentrate on her work and didn't half listen to Ms. Rosengren's presentation of the myths of ancient Greece.

Ms. Rosengren seldom bawled anybody out; she just wrote no-telling-what in her notebook. When Ali saw her making notes, she thought Ms. Rosengren deserved an explanation.

As kids pushed out of the room for lunch, Ali stopped at the teacher's desk. "Ms. Rosengren, are we still researching career goals this year?" Ms. Rosengren nodded. "I want to change mine to special reading teacher. I've got this neat method."

"You seem to be better motivated, Ali." Ms. Rosengren put her notebook away.

"You remember last year when you were counselor, I was supposed to talk to you? I didn't say much because I didn't have much to say. But now I have, because I know my mother. That's all I can think about." Ali rushed on. "I saw your picture in my mother's *Excelsior*. Did you know her?"

"As well as a freshman ever knows a senior, I guess. I remember Kathleen McNair as one of the loveliest, most talented—"

"Did you know my father, Mark Doyle, too?" Ali's voice was little more than a whisper.

"Oh, we all knew him. He made a stir when he came to St. Stephen High from Castleton. A new boy in town." Ms. Rosengren seemed more like a person than a teacher. "Of course, he didn't pay any attention to us humble freshmen."

"Why isn't his picture in the book?"

"I suppose because he came to St. Stephen High in late fall, after the deadline for turning in pictures. The *Excelsior* director was very inflexible about that. Too bad his picture isn't there. You'd see why your mother was just crazy about him." Ms. Rosengren blushed and bit her lip. "Oh, I didn't mean. . . ."

"I know; it's all right. Remember, we had that unit on verbal variables."

Ali had a lot to think about as she walked home. She recalled how she had sassed Bobbi for saying

Mark Doyle had been in her mother's class and that no one knew where he was now. Bobbi seemed to be at least half right.

Perhaps Nana might be more willing to talk about Mark Doyle these days. Ali hoped for an opportunity to ask as she helped Nana clean the kitchen.

Nana spread out new shelf paper. "I'll do what I can. A little is better than nothing, I always say, Ali, and I didn't get a lick of housecleaning done last spring. See this, looks like a rat's nest. These are recipes I've torn out of the *Sentinel.*"

They gave Ali an idea for Nana's Christmas present. She would make an indexed recipe file, which would please her. Asking about Mark Doyle wouldn't. That could wait.

She began her file that evening. She wrote *desert* for one important category. It didn't look right. There might be two *s*'s. She found *desert* in Little Web: a wild, uninhabited tract. Then her eye fell on the definition for the next word. *Desertion*: abandonment of a person to whom one is obligated by legal agreement or status. Desertion. Pop had hinted at it once when he said her father wasn't dead. She hadn't wanted to think about the possibility then, before she had seen her mother. She realized Nana wouldn't want to tell her that her father had deserted her. Nana would think she didn't understand, but she did.

Desertion must happen pretty often to be in the dictionary. So if it were true, Ali thought, she wasn't the only kid who had ever been deserted.

22

Ali brought in the mail and put it on the table beside a note that lay there. She picked up the note and read: "Gone with Pop to get groc's. If not home by 5 PM, start potatoes."

Ali looked through the envelopes. In between the mail addressed to Resident was a long white envelope for Mr. and Mrs. Thurman McNair. The return address was: Pienkowski, Social Service Department, Webbs Flats State Hospital.

Ali looked at the envelope for a long time. It didn't seem to be sealed very well. She remembered how Nana had stood at that very table and said one thing she didn't do was open other people's mail. Then Ali thought of her mother pleading to come home. Somebody had to help her. Taking the letter opener from the table drawer, she carefully

158

ran it under the flap, took out the letter, and read.

"Dear Mr. and Mrs. McNair: Kathleen continues to improve. I believe you will agree that she handled the emotional impact of seeing her daughter in a very stable manner. All of the staff here have been impressed by her energy and good attitude, particularly since your last visit.

"Her progress under a carefully controlled prescription of lithium has been remarkable. This is particularly gratifying to all of us here, since her manic-depressive psychosis was long and complex. As I explained to you, lithium has not been used in this country until recently. It seems to be as near a miracle drug as any that exists. Lithium is believed to correct chemical imbalances in certain nerve-impulse transmitters that influence emotional status and behavior. It is many months now since Kathleen required the continuous use of this medication. The possible occasional controlled use in the future does not necessitate her hospitalization.

"She needs confidence in her ability to live successfully away from the hospital. It is generally agreed here that she would benefit from a visit home with the near-future goal of discharge as soon as suitable arrangement for living in the community can be made. Appropriate aftercare would also be part of the arrangement. With your cooperation, we believe this move can be made successfully.

"I hope to hear from you very soon on plans to have her leave the hospital for an extended home visit. This would be an important first step for her and would be evidence of your confidence in her ability to adjust to a less-sheltered life."

Ali's hands shook as she held the letter. She could imagine Nana's frown line deepening when she read it. She wouldn't do anything about it. But the letter should be answered right away. Ali had to do something herself. She'd be miserable if she did nothing to help her mother.

Ali knew the form of a business letter from fifth grade. No problem there. It should be short. Business people were busy every second and hadn't time to read more than a few words.

She opened her loose-leaf notebook and wrote with her heavy felt-tip pen.

Dear Mr. Pienkowski,

We wish Kathleen to come home. My cousin, Mr. Ted Highfield, will come for her Saturday, December 7, at 10 AM o'clock.

Yours truly, Elizabeth McNair

Ali looked at her letter critically. Although it

was short and businesslike it didn't seem right. It looked as if some kid had written it on a sheet of loose-leaf paper.

A typed letter would be better. There was a typewriter in the attic. Ali remembered Nana pointing to it and saying, "That's a good typewriter. Not cheap. We got it for her to take to college."

She found sheets of plain, unlined paper on the library table. As Ali hurried up the narrow attic steps, she wondered if Nana might have sold the typewriter or donated it to the church rummage. But it was still there, far back under the low part of the roof.

She took the machine out of its dusty case and carried it to the light that shone in the attic window. Slowly hunting for each letter, she typed the message, thankful that business letters were short. Next summer she would learn to type fast. It was cold in the attic. Signing Nana's name was easy; she'd seen that signature often enough.

Finally Ali pecked out on a clean sheet of paper, "Dear Ted, Our Chevy broke down twice last week. It might not make it to Webbs Flats. Kathleen is due to come home. Please go to the hospital 10 AM o'clock Saturday, December 7, to bring her here. Please stay for lunch. Many thanks, Betty." Cousin Ted might wonder why he got a short, typed note from Nana, but Ali hoped he'd be so glad to get mail he wouldn't wonder too long.

The typewriter was replaced and Ali downstairs with the two addressed envelopes behind her back when Pop and Nana came in. Nana dropped a bag of groceries on the kitchen counter. "You didn't start the potatoes. Pop's hungry." She turned as Ali put on her jacket and thrust the letters into the pocket. "Now where are you going? I'll need help getting these groceries put away."

"Be right back!" Ali ran out the front door, jumped on her bike, and pedaled hard. Now that she had written the letters, she had to mail them before she lost her nerve.

They had finished supper before Nana got to the mail. She sighed as she read Mr. Pienkowski's letter.

"Any mail?" Pop asked, as he handed her the paper.

"Nothing to speak of. Nothing we haven't heard before." She jerked her head toward Ali in a gesture Ali recognized as meaning, Can't talk about it now.

Instead, Nana read items from the paper. "Well, it says right here, a fellow twenty-eight years old was picked up for shoplifting a cactus plant valued at forty-nine cents at C and B Cut-Rate. Seems like an odd item to pick up, hard to hide." Nana went on to another item. "Forgery . . . arraigned on a charge of forgery, pleaded not guilty, case to come before December term of court."

Forgery! The word hit Ali like a blow. She had committed a double crime. She had forged Nana's name twice. What's more, she'd put the letters in the mail. That was mail fraud, a Federal United States crime! Right now, the letters were going through the canceling machine, along with the honest mail. Ali wondered desperately if there was any way to get letters out of the post office once you got them in. If only she had talked it over with Pop, confessed she'd tampered with United States mail and opened his letter. She and Pop could have figured out what to do. But *if only* didn't help; she had sent the letters. Mail was awful slow, though, even to Webbs Flats. She could hurry and write other letters, saying the first ones were wrong. They would all be delivered at the same time.

Suddenly Ali realized she didn't want to undo what she had started. She'd done it, just the way she'd bought her own school clothes. Nana could get mad, cry, call the FBI, do whatever she wanted. It didn't matter. Ali had to be brave enough to take risks to help her mother. She was her daughter and had a legal obligation to do so.

What would Cousin Ted think of being ordered around? Ali wondered. Maybe he'd call, wanting an explanation, and Mr. Pienkowski would do the same. Ali jumped every time the phone rang. After a conversation with a church-circle friend, Nana said Ali would sprain her ears if she eavesdropped any harder.

But there was no word from anyone. It was as if Ali had never mailed those forgeries. Perhaps she hadn't licked the stamps well enough, and they'd fallen off. Sometimes letters got lost, or people paid no attention to them. Some bureaucrat, as Nana might say, probably had opened her letter, decided some kid had written it, and thrown it in the wastebasket. In that case, they could deal with Cousin Ted when he showed up.

The silence was a strain. Each day Ali checked the calendar and counted the days until December 7. Perhaps it would go by like any other Saturday, and nothing would happen. That is, if the day ever came at all.

When school started in September, Ali could never bear to think of June. It was too far away. By Tuesday, December 3, the coming Saturday seemed at least that far away. On Wednesday, December 4, it seemed even further.

Ali tried to follow Nana's advice and keep busy. She cleaned the room twice. She finished Nana's recipe file. After promising she wouldn't mess up the clean kitchen, she made a batch of brownies and put them in the freezer. It would be good to have extra—just in case.

On Friday evening Ali began to feel that she couldn't take a deep breath, but she got over it. It wouldn't help to go around gasping like a fish out of water.

23

Luckily Ali had done everything in advance, for by Saturday morning she was too excited to work. She inspected the room once more: all her clothes were hung up, the furniture dusted, the floor vacuumed, the rugs shaken. She hoped Nana wouldn't start a sewing project and spread it all over the dining room. And Pop had better stay right at home; she might need him.

Ali stationed herself at an upstairs front window to wait. The paper boy came to collect for the *Sentinel.* Mrs. Clark brought Bobbi home from baton. At ten forty-five the mail jeep stopped. Two cars passed.

Then a car pulled up to the curb. Someone got out. It was Cousin Ted, big as all outdoors. His voice was big and booming, too. "Well, you're home,

Kathleen. Same old place, no use staring at it. Let's go in. I expect Betty is waiting lunch."

Ali tried not to shake the house as she jumped with joy to see her own mother come up the front walk. She covered her mouth to quiet her squeals of delight. She wanted to rush down and welcome her with a big hug.

But there was no telling what would happen when Nana opened that front door. Ali had argued with Nana often enough, been a real Miss Back-talk, but never before had she acted as if Nana had no say-so in her own house. That was about the worst thing a person could do to Nana. She might decide Ali was worse than a two-headed rattle-snake, worse than a winter wind with a terrible chill factor.

Ali tiptoed into the hall and listened. There were no cries of greeting, just low voices.

She had a sudden impulse to flee, but there was no place to go. They were all standing at the foot of the stairs. Her own mother was home. What she had wanted for so long had happened. She'd made it happen. Now she'd go down, face Nana, and show her it was time.

Ali took a deep breath. She could do that all right. Even though her legs felt like spaghetti, they got her down the steps.

She squeezed by Ted, who took up a lot of space by the front door, to stand by Kathleen. Ted twirled his wool cap on his fat fingers. "Well, when I got your note, Betty, I just did what it said. Thought you'd be tickled. Of course, there was this big flea market at Burnt Timbers today, and I'll miss that." He turned to Pop. "Did you get the Chevy fixed?"

Pop looked mystified. "Been running like a top, even with 92,000 miles. We seem to have our wires crossed here."

"Mother, didn't you know I was coming?" Kathleen sounded so hurt that Ali impulsively threw her arms around her.

Nana sank into a chair. "I've just had the props knocked out from under me. Such a shock."

Ali had never seen Nana look so old. There were red blotches on her neck. Her frown line looked permanent. With trembling hands, Nana took off her glasses and wiped her eyes. "I think somebody interfered. Took on something she didn't understand." Nana didn't look at Ali.

"But Mr. Pienkowski told me," Kathleen said, distressed.

Pop made a noise that was supposed to be a laugh. "Those bureaucrats. They just push papers around, all that red tape. Say, we're forgetting our manners here, so taken aback to have Kathleen home. I think we should scare up a little lunch."

Ted tossed his cap onto the newel-post. "I'll say *amen* to that."

"Lunch," Nana repeated, as if she'd never heard of such a thing.

Ali slipped into the kitchen and motioned to Pop to follow. "I think Nana was about to open this can of tuna for sandwiches," she whispered. "See if there is another one. I'll chop up things for a tossed salad. We've got brownies."

Kathleen came into the kitchen, smiling. "I can help. Imagine! A one-family kitchen."

Nana didn't move from her chair until Pop told her lunch was ready. Ali had set the table in the dining room because Ted was company. Kathleen acted like company, too, stiff and uneasy.

Ted sat down at the table. "I hope there's no hard feelings. Hope I wasn't the one interfered."

Nana took her place. "Of course not, Ted, but somebody imposed on you, took up your time."

"Got considerable of that, but today I'll eat and run."

"Sure. Then you won't miss the flea market entirely," Nana said. "No, you just did as instructed, Ted, not like some people."

Nana hadn't looked directly at Ali once since she'd come downstairs. She talked as if she weren't there. Ali began to feel as if she didn't count, wasn't even worth scolding.

But she did count. Her mother wouldn't be home if she hadn't brought it about. She wondered what it was Nana thought she didn't understand. Ali felt happy and scared at the same time, too mixed up to try to eat. She looked around the table.

The red blotches had faded from Nana's neck. Her hands were steady as she unfolded her paper napkin. Ali could see Nana was recovering. Probably she had thought of a plan; she might jump up and telephone Mr. Pienkowski any minute.

Kathleen reached over and grasped Ali's hand. "I've thought about this so often," she said. "Not exactly this way, but about coming home. So often."

Pop patted Kathleen's other hand. "I know. But the main thing is you're here, you're here."

"Now what's this? A Quaker silent grace?" Ted flung out his big hands to cover Ali's and Nana's. Then Pop put his arm around Nana to complete the circle. It was enough to make everybody bawl, but Ted broke it up and dived for the sandwich plate.

When they got to dessert, Nana managed a little crooked smile as she watched Ted eat brownies.

Kathleen got up from the table and walked over to the buffet. She touched the glass candlesticks lightly. Then she went into the living room, touching things.

"Do you want to go up and see our room?" Ali

asked. "I've got it all cleaned up, and I'd like to show you this funny card I made for you when I was in first grade."

"I always thought it was the best room in the house," Kathleen said, as they went upstairs. She stood in the bedroom doorway. "The ceiling seems so low." She sat at the dressing table and gravely looked at herself in the mirror. "This is just the same."

Ali took the perfume bottle from the closet shelf. "First I want to show you this. It's kind of magic. I don't know why, but if you're feeling awful—scared or mad or anything—you smell this and you feel better."

Kathleen held the bottle in the palm of her hand. "*L'air du temps*. I had this when you were a little bit of a thing. I'd dab it on the times I was happy. Maybe I made you happy then, too."

"I don't remember it."

"I guess your nose remembers feelings your brain forgets. Brains play tricks on you sometimes." Kathleen tapped Ali's freckled nose. "Noses are more reliable."

"*L'air du temps*." Ali read the label on the bottle. She didn't know what it meant. It sounded funny. "*L'air du temps*." She giggled with relief. They had gotten through lunch. Her mother was home to share the room with her.

171

"French," Kathleen said.

That was funny, too. *"L'air du temps, l'air du temps."* Ali gasped with laughter.

Kathleen laughed, too, because Ali was shrieking so. *L'air du temps* wasn't all that funny, but Ali felt wonderful to have someone to laugh with.

"Now we'd better be sensible," Kathleen said, catching her breath. "They will wonder what's the matter with us." She stood up and looked out the window. "Those pine trees back of the shop, so tall! I remember when I could jump over them. I'd like to go out and see the yard and the shop."

"Go ahead. I have to do lunch dishes. Saturdays and Sundays are just one dish after another for me. I'm supposed to do them weekends."

In the kitchen, Nana had already taken over at the sink. She didn't look at Ali but handed her a dish towel. She spoke to the dishwater. "I was just flabbergasted. You could have knocked me over with a feather when I opened the door and there stood Kathleen."

"Are you talking to me, Nana?" Ali asked innocently.

"Yes, and I have my suspicions about what you did. We'll see about that later. She can try a short visit as long as she's here, but I don't want to put more on her than she can bear." Nana turned to

172

look at Ali. "I've been through a lot, and so has she. I faced facts long ago."

"Nana, I don't know what you mean." Ali started to sniffle.

"Of course not, so you interfere."

"But she's so much better now. Things don't always stay the same. She needs us. I need her." Ali stopped, stiffened her back, and took the whine out of her voice. "When I sent a present she liked, she said it was like a miracle to know me, so I want to be a part of the miracle of making her real for me. It was as if she was dead, and I helped make her alive. I'm not sorry."

"So now you're a miracle worker. We'll see about that. Sh-h-h, she's coming in now."

24

Although Kathleen protested that she was not one bit tired, Nana insisted that she take a rest after the excitement of coming home. Nana went upstairs for a nap, too.

The house became too quiet, and Ali ran out to the shop. Pop was putting wood in the stove when she came in. "Well, Ali, you got your mother home. Cousin Ted got a note from Nana that she never wrote, and I guess the hospital people got one, too."

"Nana is making her take a nap," Ali said.

Pop looked out the window toward the house. "Sure seems natural for Kathleen to be up there in her room."

"Nana says it's only for a short visit. What do you say, Pop, or don't you have any say?"

"You bet your boots I do, and I think it's past time

I said it." Pop sat down in the rocking chair and took Ali's hand. "My old school friend Henrietta Kneehoff called me not long ago. She told me it was high time we were fair with you, said you could handle it. I know we've been closemouthed, but I didn't want to push Nana right after she'd been in the hospital."

"What promise did you make Nana? You said you'd tell me."

"Oh, I made a lot of them, Ali, like the one for better or for worse, and the worse came when Kathleen had this nervous breakdown in her late teens. You'd better sit down there on my work stool. I might be long-winded." Pop silently rocked in his old oak chair, collecting his thoughts.

"About that promise," Ali prompted.

"Long before that, Kathleen was always special. Nana's the kind of woman thought she'd have at least half a dozen young 'uns, but we only had Kathleen. So Nana wanted the best for her. She started saving up for her to go to college. Kathleen was good at drawing; that's what she liked to do. Nana wanted her to go off to college and learn to be an artist.

"Then in her last year of high school she couldn't stop talking about this Mark Doyle. He wasn't a bad guy—tall, nice-looking, happy-go-lucky kind. We knew they were going together, but we didn't think much about it. Kathleen did, though. She just couldn't get over it—that with all the girls running after him, he'd pick her. She'd always been quiet and spent a lot of time at her books. Well, naturally he felt fine that a smart girl like Kathleen thought he was perfect.

"Then when she finished high school, she came and told us she was going to marry this Doyle. Nana thought they weren't right for each other and not ready to settle down, but there was no way we could talk them out of it. The day Kathleen was eighteen they went down to the courthouse and got a marriage license.

"Mark could get work, and they had a little apartment down on River Street. Still, things didn't seem to be going right even before you were born. Mark's friends went off to college or else in the service. He said he wasn't sure he wanted to be a husband and father. You couldn't really blame the boy too much because Kathleen had changed. She wasn't herself.

"One day she'd think she could do everything, and she'd rave about all kinds of wild schemes. She'd talk a blue streak, stay up all night working, scrubbing that little place, drawing weird pictures. Next day she wouldn't do a hand's turn, wouldn't move or say a word. Mark's life was hell on earth . . . so he left."

Ali imagined a handsome, tall, happy-go-lucky fellow, not a bad guy, who was the father she'd never know. "Desertion, is that what they call it, Pop?" she whispered. The words would hardly come out.

He nodded. "We wanted Kathleen to come home, but she was too proud. I told Nana that Kathleen was near a breakdown and needed help, but Nana was proud, too—too proud to admit that, not for a girl she'd raised. I believe she was even afraid of what the neighbors would think.

"We went to see Kathleen one cold January Sunday. She seemed better, and I began to think like Nana that she was pulling out of her trouble. She had the little place looking nice; you were bathed and fed. She'd made some cookies, and she passed them around.

"Next day Nana went there and found you alone and screaming. She found a note, too. Kathleen wrote that she was going to drown herself in the St. Stephen River."

Ali was trembling so much that her teeth chattered.

"Somebody saw her and put a stop to that," Pop continued. "We got her to a doctor, and he said Kathleen should go to Webbs Flats. Nana was still bullheaded, wouldn't give in. Kathleen didn't want to go to Webbs Flats either. She wanted to be in that little apartment when Mark came back. But he didn't come . . . and she tried it again. . . ." Pop was choking on his words.

"I understand, Pop. You don't have to talk about it anymore."

"I want you to know she was dangerous to herself and to you, too. So finally Nana said, all right, she'd sign for Kathleen to be—well, to go in. She said it was the hardest thing she'd ever done, and she didn't want to do it but once.

"'Promise me,' she said, 'that you accept this as her fate and our fate. That you won't try to bring her out where she could be harmed by herself or by anyone else again.' So I promised."

Pop stumbled out of his chair to the window. His back was toward Ali, and his stooped shoulders shook as he stood there.

"Pop, why are we crying?" Ali asked shakily. "She's home now, and that was a long, long time ago."

After a while Pop spoke again. "All that time, Nana couldn't change, Ali. When she finally gave in and agreed to let Kathleen be treated, she seemed to give all in. She gave up and resigned herself that Kathleen would never be different. That's the way it used to be. People went in, and most of them stayed year after year. We had you to think about, to bring up. In time, you get used to things not being perfect, things breaking down, working only halfway."

"But things mend and grow, get better, get well," Ali objected.

"Yes. I guess that's what I forgot, and Nana couldn't believe. She let her hopes slip away. But hope is so precious that you must hold on to it for dear life. I began to get mine back after I talked to Henrietta and after that last visit when you went with us to the hospital. The doctor really lit into Nana."

"What did he say?"

"He claimed that without realizing it she didn't want Kathleen to get well and leave the hospital. After all these years, it would mean a big change in Nana's life for her to come back to St. Stephen. She had another girl now. Kathleen might take you away from us. He talked to her like a Dutch uncle."

"That was plenty mean."

"Nana was mad as a wet hen, I'll tell you. He wanted to upset her arrangements, but now you've done that, Ali. And believe me, it takes a lot of spunk to stand up to Nana. You're still a fighter."

Ali took a long, deep breath. "Thank you, Pop. You told me sad things, but I'm glad you've told me. I feel like one piece now, not a bunch of wonderings. I know as much about Ali Doyle as anyone in St. Stephen does. Maybe more, because I know my mother's home." Ali saw a light go on in the kitchen. "Nana's up. Guess I'll have to set the table, same as any other day."

But Ali couldn't go right into the house. She walked down the hill and along the park, thinking of all the things Pop had told her. They were things that had troubled her as long as she could remember. She felt better now. Knowing made a difference.

When she got home, Nana was putting a roast in the oven. Ali took four plates from the cabinet. "I'm doing this early," she said to Nana's back. "Then I can peel potatoes. There's something I have to tell you. I guess you know I wrote to Cousin Ted, Nana, but that's not all. I wrote a forgery to Mr. Pienkowski and put your name on it. Are you going to tell him?"

"Might not," Nana answered without turning around. "No need to advertise family situations."

25

Ali was happy that there was a big project under way at school. In the general confusion, she could glide through the day without much effort and hurry home to get better acquainted with her mother.

The sixth grades of the four elementary schools in St. Stephen were putting on the Combined Fine Arts Holiday Festival. So far, Ms. Rosengren was inflexible about one thing. They had to enjoy the process; the product was not so important as the process, she said.

Bobbi and Diane were practicing a baton-twirling duet. Ali was in a mural-painting group headed by Bryan Jones. He wanted to paint the history of the whole world. They'd never get it done, but Ali didn't care.

One afternoon, as she hurried home up the hill,

she was delighted to see Nana and her mother coming to meet her. Nana could hardly keep up with Kathleen, even going downhill. "Whew," she gasped, "that's enough sprinting for one day. I'm tuckered out. You and Ali can go on, Kathleen. You might want to visit the library. It's quite a ways, though; too bad you can't drive."

"I'm pretty sure I could still drive."

"You don't have a license," Nana reminded her.

"I forgot about needing a license," Kathleen said, as she and Ali started toward town. "I haven't had to think about any of those things for so long—not about what to have for supper, or who's my dentist, or anything. It scares me to think of taking care of myself."

Ali remembered how she had felt when she first went to the bank. "I'll help you get used to things," she said.

"I know you can. You've had more responsibility than I was given at your age. They certainly have let you do more."

"*Made* me do a lot of them," Ali bragged. "Had to shop and cook when Nana was operated on. I paid bills and even went to the bank. I know all about banks."

"All that know-how will help me get used to living away from Webbs Flats. I'm scared, but I'm going to try. I've got to. I've missed so much time with you. I don't even know about your nickname. I saw this movie at Webbs Flats with Ali MacGraw as star. Do they call you Ali because you look like her?"

Ali shrugged. "I guess so."

They passed the big houses on Main Street and came to St. Stephen Public Library. Kathleen looked up at the ornate cornice. "I always liked this building, inside and out. It seemed so grand, with its stone carvings."

"They built it when they still trimmed buildings," Ali said.

"Well, let's go in and see if they have any new books since I was here last." Ali liked to hear her mother laugh.

Ali couldn't leave school on time Wednesday, for Bryan Jones insisted that their group stay and work on the mural. In Miss Kneehoff's office, she called home to explain her lateness.

"Hello," her mother answered. The sound of her voice made Ali feel happy.

"Hello," the voice repeated.

"Oh, I'll be a little late," Ali stammered. "I've never heard you on the telephone before."

There was a moment of silence on the line. "I've never heard you before either, Ali. You sound wonderful to me, just wonderful. Come when you can.

Mr. Pienkowski was in St. Stephen today, and he came by. I'll tell you and Pop about it when you get home."

Ali hoped the social worker's coming had nothing to do with that business letter she'd written him.

When she got home, Kathleen explained that Mr. Pienkowski came often to St. Stephen. He visited people who had once been patients at Webbs Flats and now lived in a big house on South Range. He'd taken Kathleen and Nana to see the house, and not one word had been said about Ali's business letter.

"What did you think of the place over on South Range, Kathleen?" Pop asked.

"I thought it was really nice, friendly. People living there help each other. We saw a few, but most work during the day. The doctors from Webbs Flats come over, too, if anyone needs a doctor or has to have their medicine checked. It's called a halfway house," Kathleen explained. "People there don't have to be in the hospital, but they need a special place for a while until they get used to life in town again. Then usually they get their own apartment or house."

Nana hadn't said anything, but her frown line was showing clearly. "What do you think, Nana?" Ali asked.

"What do *I* think?" Nana sniffed. "Since when

did anyone care what I think? Noway house, I call it."

"Maybe I can see it Saturday. You know, that's when we're going to look around St. Stephen," Ali said.

Friday Ali worked overtime on the mural so she could have Saturday free.

Her mother seemed to be asleep when Ali woke up Saturday morning, so she slipped out of bed and went downstairs to set the breakfast table.

"Kathleen, breakfast is ready," Nana called. There was no response. "Go up and rouse her, Ali. This oatmeal will get cold."

Ali was so happy that she raced up the steps, two at a time, and ran down the hall to the bedroom. There was a big lump under the covers. Kathleen was still in bed with the sheet pulled over her face. Strands of dark hair were all that showed on the pillow.

Kathleen stirred and mumbled wearily, "I can't get up today. I don't feel like it. I'll have to stay in bed."

"Are you sick at your stomach or what? Want me to take your temperature?" Ali asked anxiously.

"No, I'm just tired. You can pull down the blinds."

"But it's daytime! The day we're going on our St. Stephen tour. If we start early, we can hike out to see my willow tree."

"I can't go."

Nana waited at the foot of the stairs as Ali slowly came down. She gave Nana the frightening report. "She doesn't want to get up." Just six easy words, the kind she'd taught Jonathan, but now they seemed dreadful.

Nana pushed past her. "I'll go up and see what I can do." Ali huddled on the bottom step and listened for Nana's efforts. Now and then low voices broke the long silences from the shared room.

Nana bustled downstairs and into the kitchen, where Pop waited at the table before a bowl of cold oatmeal. "Thurman, I think we'll have to take Kathleen back to Webbs Flats today. She's still in bed—not a thing wrong with her—and she won't get up. The visit is over. They know how to manage this at the hospital. That's where she should be now. I'll call over there so they will expect her."

"Wait a little, Betty," Pop said. "See how she feels by noon."

"I don't think it will be any different by noon. We've seen this before, Thurman. She's fine, then *whish*—collapse."

It took more nerve than Ali had just then to dispute Nana. She was not a miracle worker, after all. Ali was tired of trying. She just wanted to get away from the house and all its problems. She'd go down to Clarks'. After Bobbi's baton lesson, they could play Barbie dolls the rest of the day. She went to the rack to get her jacket. Nana and Pop would be relieved to have her out of the way while they took her mother back to Webbs Flats where she'd stay on and on.

But she couldn't bear to think of that happening, not now that she knew her mother, had heard her laugh. Ali mustered up some precious hope.

She replaced her jacket on the hook. "Nana, I don't think you should be so up-tight because she didn't jump out of bed like a hunter on the first day of deer season."

"Oh, don't you?"

"No, because just about everybody sleeps in once in a while."

"I don't."

"Maybe you ought."

"It's no time for impudence, Ali. This is serious and you know it. You meant well when you wrote those letters—I know that—but she can't stay. It's too much for her. If you go talk to her, I think she'll tell you so herself."

Ali sat on the side of the bed, wondering how to talk to a tuft of hair. When Kathleen finally pushed the covers aside, Ali saw a sad face.

"I'm sorry to disappoint you, Ali, but I don't want to think about all the hard things I'd have to do if I lived in St. Stephen again. It would be easier for

187

me to go back to the hospital. You can come see me there. It's like home to me. I was there so many years." Kathleen looked out at the pine trees. "I didn't grow like those pine trees or like you, and I shouldn't pretend I did."

"Listen, there's something I want to tell you." Ali looked straight at her mother. "It's about my nickname. Nobody in the entire world ever thought I looked one bit like Ali MacGraw. It's after Muhammad Ali, the prizefighter. I got in a school fight last year.

"Remember I told you about our art mural? Bryan Jones is chairman. He knows everything. He brought in a picture of this old-time church column, way back before Columbus. It showed some people stomping on an ugly creature. I thought it was the devil, but Bryan said that creature stood for despair. Even way back then, people were fighting off despair. Maybe you can't really stomp on it, but you can remember that it will go. You can feel really rotten, and a little later you can feel so much better. Then you wonder, What was that all about?"

"Not for me, Ali. I wanted to leave the hospital, to come home, but it won't work." Kathleen sat up in bed and grasped Ali by the shoulders. "Nana has never forgiven me! I know she hasn't. I am not the kind of daughter she wanted. I didn't go to college, I couldn't keep a husband, I got sick, I couldn't take care of my baby. She hasn't forgiven me, she doesn't trust me. Never once while I've been here has she let me go anywhere by myself. She hasn't forgiven me," Kathleen moaned.

She looked so forlorn that Ali had to think of something. "Nana hasn't forgiven you? Well, why don't you forgive her?"

Kathleen stared at Ali. "What did you say? Me forgive Nana?"

"Might as well. Please try, try hard."

Kathleen was sitting up in bed and seemed to be thinking hard when Ali left.

Nana was putting her sewing machine away when Ali came into the dining room. "The day won't be as planned. I was going to make myself something to wear to the school doings. Now I'll have to go to Webbs Flats. She isn't coming down, is she?"

"I don't know, Nana. Have I made everything worse?"

"Oh, no, Ali. Of course, it's awful disheartening, especially at your age. Why, I even got my hopes up a time or two, having her here. You tried to help."

"Does she have to go back right away?"

"No particular rush, I guess, but I have to keep busy. If I just sit and wait, I'll get the heebie-jeebies. We've got more kitchen cupboards to clean."

They had finished two long shelves and started

on the little spice shelf when they heard the shuffle of slippers on the stair. Kathleen wore Nana's ready-made robe, which she had lent her. "I thought I'd better have breakfast and then help Ali with the dishes," she said, as she came into the kitchen.

"Oh, I'm so glad you're feeling better!" Ali exclaimed.

"I had something to decide," Kathleen said, "and I want to tell you about it. I'm not going back to the hospital. I'm going to live at halfway house." She looked directly at Nana. "No, we aren't going to see about that. I've decided."

"I didn't say one thing," Nana protested. "Everybody gets a little backset occasionally. I'm tickled pink that you've perked up. I'll go tell Thurman. He's out in the shop, waiting to know the schedule."

"I want to show you where I'll live, Ali," Kathleen said. "I ought to be able to get myself organized so we can go over there sometime today."

"When you're ready, you two go on," Nana said at the back door. "Then I'll get back to my sewing. I'm going to try one of those double-knit pants suits for myself."

After the dishes were done, Ali continued cleaning shelves alone. The little spice cans were an awful jumble, and so were Ali's feelings. She was glad her mother was up, moving about their room. At the same time, she was sorry that her mother would not live with them, after all. Ali arranged the spice cans in alphabetical order and wished she could straighten out her feelings as easily. At least, figuring out what should come after sesame seeds got her thoughts on something else.

It was midafternoon by the time Kathleen was ready for their walk. When they went outside, Ali looked back at the house. "What about our shared room?"

"I can't come home and be Pop and Nana's little girl again, Ali."

Ali was disappointed, but she knew what her mother said was true. Kathleen couldn't come back and live in that room again and have Nana telling her when she had to take a nap.

Then Ali had an idea. "You and I could have a little house and a big yard, where I could raise warty pumpkins. If I had an office room, I could learn to type fast."

"Not right away, Ali. The hospital wouldn't okay that. It will be all I can do to take care of myself for a while. I think you know how important this week has been to me. You had faith in me, even in my ability to forgive. You gave me more confidence than the doctor or Mr. Pienkowski or anybody." Kathleen strode along, swinging her arms. "I feel so much better than I did this morning."

Ali skipped to keep up. She couldn't stay disappointed when her mother said things like that. "Will you come weekends and stay in our room with me?"

"Oh, sure. I'll help you with all those dishes."

At school, Ali worked hard on the mural, and they managed to get up to 1590 AD. Miss Kneehoff came to each room and asked the pupils whose parents were coming to the Combined Fine Arts Holiday Festival to raise their hands. Ali waved her hand and stood up. "My mother, grandfather, and grandmother are coming." She thought there was a faint glow in Miss Kneehoff's pale eyes.

At the final work session, Bryan said, "I thought your mother was—well, sick."

"She was, but she got well."

Ali wondered how six ordinary words could say so much.